# Marlo Thomas and Friends

# Thanks & Giving
## All Year Long

Edited by Marlo Thomas and Christopher Cerf

Consulting Editor: Bruce Kluger

Contributing Editor: Wendy Goldwyn Batteau

Designer: Dan Potash

SIMON & SCHUSTER BOOKS FOR YOUNG READERS

New York • London • Toronto • Sydney

## OTHER BOOKS BY MARLO THOMAS
### Free to Be . . . You and Me
### Free to Be . . . a Family
### The Right Words at the Right Time

SPECIAL THANKS

to Janet Chan, Phil Donahue, David Gale, Alene Hokenstad, Tina Keane, Audrey Kluger, Bridgette Kluger, Gary Knell, Elizabeth Law, Debra Newman, Paige Peterson, Maureen Reilly, Rick Richter, Kim Shefler Rodriguez, Anne Scatto, Gail Solow, Lee Wade,

and to

Bob Levine,

who once again proved to be our legal champion, our chief navigator, and our treasured friend.

Musical scores for this book prepared and edited by Dan Sovak

St. Jude Children's
Research Hospital

Marlo Thomas and Friends have contributed all royalties from *Thanks & Giving: All Year Long* to St. Jude Children's Research Hospital, founded by Ms. Thomas's father, Danny Thomas, in 1962.

SIMON & SCHUSTER BOOKS FOR YOUNG READERS
An imprint of Simon & Schuster Children's Publishing Division
1230 Avenue of the Americas, New York, New York 10020

# ReAd Me FiRsT!

My father used to tell me that there are two kinds of people in the world: the takers and the givers. The takers sometimes eat better, he would say, but the givers always sleep better.

My father's words began to bounce around in my head as I started work on this book. And, as they kept bouncing and bouncing, I soon got the idea that I wanted to call it *Thanks & Giving*.

I've always loved Thanksgiving. I remember my family's lively dinner conversations, the wonderful smell of sweet potatoes, and the fun and games we kids had once we'd talked the grown-ups into letting us leave the table the second we finished our pumpkin pie.

I also love that the word "Thanksgiving" brings together two great ideas—*thanks* and *giving*— that we can celebrate every day of the year.

Every day we can stop for a second and be thankful for all those things in our lives, both large and small, that make us who we are: family, friendship, laughter, music, hope, magic, love. (As you'll see in this book, we can even be thankful for a million tiny things that we often forget about, like zippers, bottle caps, and galoshes!)

As for the giving part, all you need to do is remember the feeling you get when you make your grandmother a birthday card, or share a doughnut with your little brother, or teach your cousin a silly song, or even hug a friend hello, to know that giving comes as naturally to all of us as smiling. And who doesn't know how to smile?

So you see, we thank and give every day.

What follows on these pages are stories, poems, and songs by writers and illustrators whose work you've known since before you could even read. This book also includes some wonderful tales written by people you may have seen on TV or in the movies. All of these contributors have generously reached back into their childhoods, or into their imaginations, for a special moment to share with you.

And here's another wonderful thing about the book you now hold in your hands: Just by having it, you are already giving. Because whether you bought it on your own, or it was given to you as a gift, all of the royalties go to St. Jude Children's Research Hospital, where doctors and scientists work hard every day to make very sick kids better.

And, of course, my real hope for *Thanks & Giving* is that it will help remind all of us to be thankful for the children in our lives who are healthy, and to give to the children who are not, so that someday *all* kids will be healthy.

Now, remember what I told you my father said about "givers" at the beginning of this page? (You can peek, go ahead.) Then all I have left to say is . . .

Sleep well.

(But before you turn off the light, turn the page and enjoy what my friends and I have created for you.)

*Marlo Thomas*

For
The Children
of
St. Jude Children's Research Hospital
and
Their Parents

# CONTENTS

# THE MOUSE, THE BIRD, AND THE SAUSAGE

## (A Not-Often-Told Grimm's Fairy Tale)

### retold by Jon Scieszka and illustrated by Lane Smith

Way back in the old days, a mouse, a bird, and a sausage lived happily together. Each worked a different job, and they got along wonderfully.

Every day the mouse fetched a pot of water.

Every day the bird gathered wood for the fire.

Every day the sausage used the water to make soup, and then swam around in it to add a bit of flavor.

Life was good.

But you know how it is—when people are doing well, they still seem to wish for something more.

So one morning Bird started complaining. "Mouse, you have such an easy job. You fetch one pot of water in the morning. Then you take the rest of the day off."

"So?" said Sausage to Bird. "All you do is pick up a few twigs."

"Oh, yeah?" said Bird. "Come to think of it, you probably do the least, Sausage. You just swim around a bit."

"I'd like to see you do my job," said Sausage.

"I'd like to see you do my job," said Mouse.

"I'd like to see you do my job," said Bird.

Mouse, Bird, and Sausage argued and argued until they finally agreed to settle the matter by switching jobs.

Sausage went out to collect wood. He ran into a dog, who decided to have him for breakfast, and was never seen again.

Bird went to fetch a pot of water. He fell down the well, couldn't fly out because his feathers got wet, and was never heard from again.

When Sausage and Bird didn't return, Mouse started a fire and heated the soup from the day before. He climbed into the pot to flavor the boiling soup and quickly lost both his hair and his life.

So give thanks for what you have and what your friends give to you. Otherwise, like Mouse, you might end up in very hot water.

# Stones
### *in a*
# Stream

by Jeff Moss

illustrated by
Barry Root

One day, millions of years ago,
As springtime turned the world green,
A boy and a dad took a long quiet walk
And stopped by the side of a stream.
The day was clear and bright and cool,
And nobody else was around.
The whoosh of the water hurrying by
Was the morning's only sound.
The boy and the dad sat still on the grass
And in silence enjoyed the day.
(Of course, back then no one knew how to talk
So there wasn't a lot to say.)
They turned and looked at the blue of the sky
And the white of some dinosaur bones,
Until their eyes fell on some dried-up sticks
And some different-sized scattered stones.

The dad gazed down. He let out a grunt,
And he moved from his resting place.
With a curious finger, he touched a stone,
And a different look crossed his face.
He turned toward the stream, and his eyes seemed to say
That he wanted to try something more.
And then the dad did a strange new thing
No one ever had done before.

The dad bent over and picked up a stone,
And he threw it into the stream.

2

Then his eyes grew wide as a circle formed
Where the stone pierced the water's gleam.
The boy and the dad stood perfectly still
As they watched the circle grow
Bigger and bigger, till it disappeared
Into dirt-brown banks below.
The dad made a sound—it was not quite a bark
And not quite a hoot of joy.
He bent down and picked up another stone,
And he handed it to the boy.

The boy took the stone and turned toward the stream;
He wanted to try it, too.
And as his dad watched, the boy raised his arm,
And he let out a cry, and he threw.
His head bounced back as he heard the splash,
And then as the circle grew wide,
The boy and dad looked at each other
And they felt something new inside.
There weren't yet words to describe what they felt;
Still somehow, the two of them knew
That in the world, there were special things
That a boy and a dad could do.

All afternoon, by the banks of the stream,
Stones skittered and plopped and skimmed,
One after another, *boom* and *kerplunk,*
As the bright sun slowly dimmed.
Flat stones and round ones, as on and on
They continued, the father and son,
Till a sliver of moon flecked the water,
And, finally, their throwing was done.
They both were happy and tired
As they quietly stood at rest.
Then slowly the dad wrapped his arms 'round the boy,
And he pulled him close to his chest.
The boy curled his arms around the dad's neck,
And they both felt safe and glad,
And that hug became the very first hug
Between a boy and a dad.

3

# A Tale of Two Friends

By JOSEPH A. BAILEY
(ADAPTED BY NORMAN STILES)
ILLUSTRATED BY JOE MATHIEU

MARLO: Once upon a time, not very long ago, there were two very best friends. As the time got closer to Christmas, the two friends found out that each had a very serious problem. While sitting in the bathtub, one friend said to himself:

BERT: La, la, la. Ah, golly wonkers, it's almost Christmas and I haven't got a thing for Ernie. *(Squeak, squeak.)* Uh oh, I just sat on something in the water! *(Squeak, squeak.)* Ah, it's Ernie's rubber duckie! It must have slipped into the water. Say, that gives me a nifty idea! I know what to get Ernie for Christmas. I'll get Ernie a soap dish to put his rubber duckie in! *(He laughs.)*

MARLO: Meanwhile, the other friend, who was eating in the kitchen, said to himself:

ERNIE: Whoops! Oh, while I was sitting here wondering what to get ole buddy Bert for Christmas, I knocked ole buddy Bert's paper-clip collection right off the kitchen table. Hey, that gives me a terrific idea! I'll get him a cigar box to keep his paper clips in. Then when I knock it down on the floor, they'll be safe. *(He giggles.)*

MARLO: Well, both friends thought all their problems were solved. Then they found they each had *another* problem. Bert said to himself:

BERT: Wait a minute! I don't have any money to buy Ernie a soap dish to put his rubber duckie in.

MARLO: And Ernie said to himself:

ERNIE: Uh-oh, I don't have any money. So how can I get a cigar box for Bert's paper-clip collection for Christmas?

MARLO: Well, it was a little later that I got into the story. I happened to be helping out in Hooper's Store for the holidays when my old friend Ernie walked in. Hi, Ernie!

ERNIE: Hi there, Marlo. Hey, that sure is a fine-looking cigar box. Don't suppose you would trade it for my rubber duckie, would you?

MARLO: Ernie! Your *rubber duckie*? Are you sure?

ERNIE: Please, Marlo. I just gotta have that cigar box!

MARLO: Well, if it's really that important to you, here's the cigar box, Ernie.

ERNIE: Thanks! Bye, Marlo. Bye, Rubber Duckie. *(He chokes back a sob.)*

MARLO: Bye, Ernie. So then, soon after Ernie traded his rubber duckie to get Bert a cigar box for Christmas, my old friend Bert walked in. Hi, Bert!

BERT: Hi, Marlo. Listen, I am prepared to offer you the deal of a lifetime. Now see this? This is the finest paper-clip collection in the Western Hemisphere. Look, here's my 1957 Acme, ah, and this one I bent in the shape of the letter *w*.

MARLO: That's very impressive, Bert.

BERT: Yeah. Now, I am prepared to trade you this terrific paper-clip collection for just one small soap dish. Well, Marlo, do we have a deal? Please!

MARLO: What can I say, Bert? You talked me into it. Here's the soap dish.

BERT: Oh, thank you, Marlo.

MARLO: You're welcome, Bert.

BERT: Bye, paper clips! *(He starts to cry.)*

MARLO: When Christmas morning came, the two friends exchanged gifts.

ERNIE: Open yours first, Bert.

BERT: Okay! *(He takes the wrapping paper off very gingerly.)* Oh, Ernie, a cigar box! That's wonderful!

ERNIE: I got it for you so you could keep your paper-clip collection in it.

BERT: What?

ERNIE: Come on, Bert, get your paper clips! I can't wait to see how they look!

BERT: Yeah, well, ah . . . Ernie, you haven't opened up *your* present yet. Come on, come on, open it up!

ERNIE: Okay, Bert. Oh, Bert, a new soap dish! That's beautiful!

BERT: I got it for Rubber Duckie so he won't keep falling into the tub and sinking. Let's see how he looks in it.

ERNIE: What?

BERT: Let's see how Rubber Duckie looks in his new soap dish!

ERNIE: Well, uh, I . . .

*(Then they hear a knock at the door.)*

ERNIE: Oh, I'll get it. Say, it's Marlo!

BERT/ERNIE: Merry Christmas, Marlo.

MARLO: Merry Christmas, Ernie. Merry Christmas, Bert. I just stopped by to drop off some Christmas presents. Here, this is for you, Bert. And this is for you, Ernie.

BERT/ERNIE: Thanks, Marlo!

ERNIE: What did you get, Bert?

BERT: Let's see. . . . It's my *paper-clip collection*! Thank you, Marlo!

ERNIE: But Bert, how did Marlo get your paper-clip collection?

MARLO: Never mind, Ernie. Just open your present.

ERNIE: Okay. . . . It's *Rubber Duckie*! Hello, Rubber Duckie! *(Squeak, squeak.)* Yes! I missed you, too!

BERT: How did Marlo get Rubber Duckie?

ERNIE: It's a long story. . . . But, oh, thank you, Marlo!

MARLO: It's okay, Ernie.

BERT: Say, Ernie, we didn't get anything for Marlo!

ERNIE: You're right, Bert.

MARLO: That's where you're wrong. I got the best Christmas present ever.

BERT: Oh, what's that, Marlo? Tell us.

MARLO: I got to see two best friends get exactly what they wanted for Christmas.

BERT: Aw, Merry Christmas, Marlo.

ERNIE: Yeah, Merry Christmas, Marlo.

MARLO: And a Merry Christmas to you.

# TEENY MEANY

## by David Slavin
## illustrated by Jimmy Pickering

Jeannie Meany was mean. Really mean. We're talking mean like you've never seen. Meaner than a tiger with a toothache. Meaner than a bear with a bellyache. Meaner than a whole herd of hippos with headaches. She woke up mean, she ate breakfast mean, she went to school mean, she drew pictures mean, she had snack mean, she read books mean, she ate lunch mean, she napped mean, she had circle time mean. . . . You get the picture. The girl was mean.

Don't believe me? Ask Sheldon's shin. Or Patty's pinky. Or Lyle's . . . well, you can't ask Lyle—he's still in the hospital.

Like I said, mean with a capital M-E-A-N.

Maybe Jeannie was mean because of her name—it was *Meany,* after all. If her name had been Jeannie Joyful, or Sunny Disposition, or Happy Rockefeller, maybe she would have been joyful or sunny or happy. Who knows?

But the bigger problem was her *nickname.* See, Jeannie Meany was—

what's a nice way to put this? She was . . . petite. Diminutive. Lilliputian. Oh, all right, she was *small*. And, kids being kids, you can imagine what they called her, can't you? Right. "Teeny Meany."

Now, most people aren't bothered by nicknames. Tall people are sometimes called "Stretch," left-handed people are called "Lefty," people named Art are called "Farty Arty," and they couldn't care less. (Well, Art probably cares.) But Jeannie Meany *hated* being called "Teeny," and it made her meaner and meaner with each passing nicknamey day. Everyone was so afraid of her, they'd run and hide whenever she came near. It didn't matter where you were—the playground, the pool, even the library. If Teeny Meany was coming, you were going.

"How can you be scared of *her*?" grown-ups would ask. "She's so . . . *tiny*."

To which the kids would always respond, "She's a mean girl in a small package."

Well, just about the time that Teeny Meany was getting close to being the meanest she'd ever been in her whole entire life, a new boy moved into town. His name was Michael McCatty and he was—what's a nice way to put this? He was . . . husky. Rotund. Portly. Oh, all right, he was *big*. And, kids being kids, you can imagine what they called him, can't you? Right again. "Fatty McCatty."

One day, Fatty McCatty was standing in line at the ice-cream truck, when who should walk up but Teeny Meany. The rest of the line moved aside lickety-split, but because Fatty McCatty had never met or even *heard* of Teeny Meany before (and because he really liked ice cream), he simply walked to the head of the line and asked for a Nutty Buddy.

"What do you think you're doing?" said Teeny Meany.

"Getting a Nutty Buddy," said Fatty McCatty.

(*"Uh-oh!"* said the kids.)

"You're in my spot," said Teeny Meany.

"No, actually, I was here first," said Fatty McCatty.

("*Oh, man!*" said the kids.)

"Do you know who I am?" asked Teeny Meany.

"No. Who are you?" replied Fatty McCatty.

("*Oh, no!*" gasped the kids.)

"I'm Jeannie Meany," said Teeny Meany.

"Nice to meet you, Jeannie. My name's Michael McCatty. I'm new in town. Want an ice cream?" said Michael.

Teeny Meany was speechless. It had been so long since anyone called her Jeannie, and even longer since anyone offered her anything out of *friendship,* that she just didn't know what to say. Here, standing before her, was a kind and gentle stranger who wanted nothing more than to make a new friend and buy that friend an ice cream.

Teeny Meany thought back on all of the teasing she had put up with over the years, and all of the loneliness she felt as everyone became more and more afraid of her. And she looked up at this new boy—this warm and tender soul—and said:

"Move it, Fatty."

I told you she was mean.

# AN ATTITUDE OF GRATITUDE

WORDS BY BRUCE HART AND MUSIC BY CHRISTOPHER CERF
ILLUSTRATED BY S. D. SCHINDLER

Bully in the playground.
Where'm I gonna play?
Found a better playground
half a block away.

Made a little song up.
Caught a little rhyme.
An attitude of gratitude
will do it every time.

10

# AN ATTITUDE OF GRATITUDE

Words by BRUCE HART
Music by CHRISTOPHER CERF

# The Birthday Doll

*by* Gail Carson Levine

*illustrated by* Dan Andreasen

This is a real memory. It all happened, right down to the doll's white ankle socks.

On my fourth birthday I came down with a sore throat and a high fever. My mother and father had to cancel my party. I was too sick to care, but they felt awful for me.

Sometime in the evening they brought a huge gift-wrapped box into my room. Inside the box was a doll my grandfather, Mom's father, had bought for me.

Dad held it up to show me. It was the best doll I'd ever owned. It had everything, even eyelashes. Not only eyelashes, but also eyelids that opened and closed over its bright blue eyes. Its cheeks were round and rosy, and its bright pink lips were parted in a half smile. It had stiff, golden blond hair. Later, when I touched the hair, I could feel each strand.

The doll was almost as big as I was. There was nothing cuddly about it. The face and body were hard plastic. There were joints at the shoulders and hips. You could raise the doll's arm or make it walk, although it lumbered like Frankenstein's monster.

Mom told me the doll was beautiful. She said its outfit was adorable. It wore a red-and-white polka-dot dress with puffed sleeves. Mom pointed out the white ankle socks and the red Mary Janes.

Dad said I was a lucky girl to be given such a beautiful doll.

Mom said I should take good care of the doll when I was well enough to play with it.

I began to not like it much.

Dad added I should take better care of it than I took of my other toys.

Mom said I had to play with it gently.

Dad said I would be very bad if I broke it.

I hated it.

They stood it in a place of honor on top of my dresser and admired it some more. My mother fluffed out its skirt. My father raised its arm and made it wave good night to me. They kissed me and left the bedroom.

In a few days I recovered from my illness, and then I destroyed the doll as quickly as I could. I left it out on our fire escape in the rain. I stored it at the bottom of my toy box and piled my other toys on top. I got sandbox sand in its joints.

I don't recall being punished for ruining the doll, but I do recall feeling horribly guilty—and glad at the same time.

Years passed, and I grew up. When I was thirty-eight, my father died. A year later, my mother died. Not long after that, I became interested in writing for children. Maybe because I missed Mom and Dad so much, I wanted to write about things that had happened to me when I was little.

I thought of the birthday doll and decided to visit that memory. I used a concentration technique to get myself back to it. I sat and closed my eyes. I made myself feel sluggish and heavy. I imagined a tunnel. I imagined plodding through the tunnel to the memory at the other end.

When I arrived in our old apartment, I was no longer the bedridden child with the fever-flushed face and the fever-bright eyes. Now I was an invisible presence.

There was my mother. Her hair was its original brown, and she wasn't as skinny as she became later on. There was my father, wearing his beige cardigan. His hair was still brown, too, and he had more of it than I remembered. The doll was in his arms. They were both looking at it.

For the first time I saw it as they had.

You see, Mom adored her father, who wasn't wealthy. In fact, he was poor. Such a high-quality doll would have been a big expense for him. Mom was surprised and touched by his generosity. The doll was precious to her because it was a sign of his love. That's why she wanted me to take good care of it.

Dad was marveling at my good fortune. He'd been an orphan and had grown up in an orphanage. He was thinking how well he'd have treated his toys, if he'd had any.

The memory ended. I was back in the present. I had learned why they'd lectured me about the doll.

I want to be very clear: I had good reason to be angry and even to hate the doll. I'm sorry I destroyed it, but I understand why I did. I think Mom and Dad should have given me the freedom to enjoy my present in any way I liked. I would have loved the doll then.

So I was wrong and right at the same time. My mother and father were wrong and right at the same time, too. We were all wrong and all right, each of us for different reasons.

And in the end the doll turned out to be a magnificent present. It took me back to Mom and Dad. Thank you, birthday doll.

# Give and Take

by Maurice Sendak

# A Different Aladdin

BY NORMAN STILES
ILLUSTRATED BY JIMMY PICKERING

Once there was this guy named Aladdin. Not *that* Aladdin. That Aladdin had no stuff, no stuff at all. *This* Aladdin was different. This Aladdin *had* stuff.

Stuff like a red bicycle with a small dent in the fender, a soccer ball that was autographed by a really famous soccer player and had a stain of some kind on it, a cowboy hat with no feather in the hatband . . . some pretty nice stuff.

You'd think that having some pretty nice stuff would have made Aladdin happy. But you'd be wrong. It didn't, so he wasn't. "Some" stuff wasn't good enough for Aladdin.

"If I had a *lot* of stuff, maybe I'd be happy," he told his mother.

And he sighed a deep sigh, frowned a sad frown, and started moping around the house.

Now, when I say Aladdin moped around the house, I mean exactly that. He actually went outside and walked in a circle around his house, all the while repeating the word "mope" over and over again. "Mope, mope, mope!" he said. "Mope, mope, mope, mope, mope!"

Of course, this upset Aladdin's mother quite a bit. She wanted her son to be happy and smiling.

"Okay," she said. "You say having a lot of stuff might make you happy? Then I will get you a lot of stuff!" And she wasn't kidding around. She got Aladdin all the stuff she could afford. And when she ran out of money, she sold the car, their house, and even her favorite earrings so she could get him even *more* stuff.

She got him a new bicycle *without* a dent, a new autographed soccer ball *without* stains, and a cowboy hat *with* a feather in its hatband. And that was just for starters. . . .

I could tell you everything she bought him, but that would take way too long. Let's just say that she got Aladdin so much stuff that it would have been totally impossible to fit it all into their house . . . if they still had one.

Aladdin's mom was sure that he'd be happy now. But he wasn't.

"Mom," Aladdin said, "you've gotten me a *lot* of stuff, and I really appreciate it. But I'm still not happy! Of course, maybe I *would* be happy if I had a lot *more* stuff. . . ."

And then he said, "Excuse me, Mom, I've got to go do that sighing, frowning, moping thing again, if it's okay with you."

"No problem," his mother said. "In fact, I think I'll join you."

And she did. But because they no longer had a house, they had to mope around the pile of stuff, which was now as big as their house used to be. "Mope, mope, mope!" they said. "Mope, mope, mope, mope, mope!"

Just then an old man with a long gray beard flew in on an ancient-looking magic carpet. "I saw a story on the news about a kid who had a lot of stuff but thought he needed *more* stuff to be happy," the man said, "and I wanted to help out."

He tossed a grungy old oil lamp, made of brass, to Aladdin. "It's not much, kid, but it's all I've got,"

he said, and then he flew off in a cloud of dust.

Aladdin's mother coughed and said, "He should vacuum that carpet more often."

"He should clean his lamps once in a while, too," Aladdin added. And he started rubbing the lamp.

The lamp shook and glowed and made some pretty weird noises and out came a genie.

"I am the genie of the lamp!" the genie declared. "See, it says so on my name tag."

"Wow, a genie! Now I can wish for enough stuff to make me happy!" Aladdin exclaimed to his mother, who just stood there with her mouth open, speechless.

"Hold on," said the genie. "I didn't come here to grant your wish."

"What?" said Aladdin. "What kind of genie doesn't grant wishes?"

"A genie who already gave away all his wishes. *That's* what kind of genie. I'm tapped out. No wishes left. Sorry."

"Then why *did* you come?" Aladdin asked.

"Well, actually, I wanted to ask if you would mind granting *my* wish," the genie said, very nicely.

Now *both* Aladdin and his mother were standing there with their mouths open, speechless.

"I'll take that as a yes," the genie said, and then he told Aladdin his wish. "Oh, great Aladdin, Aladdin with a lot of stuff . . . I wish I had a bicycle. I never had one."

Aladdin snapped out of it. "You never had a bicycle?" he asked.

"Never one of my own," said the genie. "Please grant my wish. One without dents would be nice. You don't have to, of course. Only if it will make you happy."

Aladdin didn't think that giving away a bike would make him happy, but he shrugged and gave the new bike without dents to the genie anyway.

"Thank you, Aladdin. Thank you," the genie

said. And then he hugged Aladdin, jumped on the bike, and started riding around, doing wheelies. "My very own bike!" he cried. "Whee!"

A strange, new expression suddenly flickered on Aladdin's face, and the sight of it was enough to shock his mother back to her senses.

"Is that a smile?" she marveled, pausing only to spit out a mosquito that had flown into her mouth while it was open.

"Could be," he answered. "You know, I kinda *liked* giving away that bicycle."

Just then the genie rode up to Aladdin, hugged him again, and said, "Toodle-oo! Gotta go. You have filled my genie heart with joy!" And he started to ride back into the lamp.

Aladdin was crestfallen. "Wait!" he yelled. "Don't you want to wish for more stuff?"

"No, thanks," the genie said. "You've given me more than enough." And he was gone.

Aladdin sighed a deep sigh and frowned a sad frown.

"If I could give away more stuff, I'd be happy," he said to his mother. And you guessed it. He started moping around the pile of stuff again. "Mope, mope, mope! Mope, mope, mope, mope, mope!"

"Stop moping!" cried Aladdin's mother, surprised by the new strength in her voice. "You say giving away more stuff will make you happy? Well then, go find some folks who have little or no stuff, and give stuff to them!"

And that's exactly what Aladdin did. Before long, he had given away so much stuff that it was easy to fit what was left into their house . . . which he was able to buy back for his mother, along with her car and her favorite earrings, because he returned the rest of the new stuff she'd bought for him and got a refund.

Aladdin's mother was overwhelmed with gratitude. "But," she said, "all you have left is the dented bicycle, the stained soccer ball, the featherless cowboy hat . . . basically the same stuff you had before this story started. Are you happy now?"

"Mom," he said, "I don't see how I could be any happier."

Just then a little girl and her mother walked by, carrying lots and lots of shopping bags. Aladdin heard the little girl say to her mother, "If I had a lot more stuff, maybe I'd be happy."

The little girl sighed a deep sigh, frowned a sad frown, and said, "Let's hurry home so I can mope around the house."

The little girl and her mother were walking as fast as they could, but before they had gotten very far, a boy wearing a cowboy hat with no feather rode up to them on a dented bicycle.

"I couldn't help but overhear that you wanted more stuff," the boy said, reaching into his bicycle basket, "and I'd like to help out." From underneath a soccer ball with a stain on it, he pulled out an old brass lamp, and tossed it to the little girl.

"It's not much," he said, "but it just might solve your problem." And he rode off in a cloud of dust.

"Hey, he got dust all over my new lamp!" the little girl complained to her mother. And she started rubbing the lamp.

# A SMILE CONNECTS US

by *Carol Hall*    illustrated by *Joe Mathieu*

A smile's as quiet
As a breath of air.
It says hello,
I'm here . . . you're there.
If you're feeling friendly,
Then a friend I'll be.
A smile connects us,
You and me.

A smile's as simple
As a moon in space.
It fills a room,
It lights a face.
It's a kind of message
Anyone can send.
A smile connects us,
Friend to friend.

This planet sometimes seems a lonely world,
As we go traveling to find the things we seek.
Try to remember it's our only world
And a smile can be the language
Anyone can learn to speak.

A smile is stronger
Than a bridge of steel.
It says the kindly
Things we feel.
And it's easy giving,
And the gift is free.
A smile connects us,
A smile connects us,
A smile connects us,
You and me.

# Letters to My Brother . . .

## julianne moore

Dear Peter,

When you were seven we used to call you "Lucky Pierre." That's because you were always finding things on the floor. Sometimes it was a dime or a quarter; other times a little toy soldier. Maybe it's because you were little and so close to the ground.

One day you and Valerie and I were playing outside, and you came running over to us, all excited. You'd found a twenty-dollar bill in a parking lot near our house! You were jumping up and down, going on and on about it. But before you could figure out what you wanted to do with your newfound treasure, Valerie and I decided for you.

See, you may not remember this, but Valerie and I could always get you to do whatever we wanted you to do. Most big sisters are like that, and we were <u>really</u> good at it.

So we told you that the best thing you could do with your twenty dollars . . . <u>was to take the whole family out for pizza</u>!

"Mom wouldn't have to cook," we said to you. "It will make her <u>so</u> happy!"

Of course, our real reason for asking you to take the family to dinner didn't have a thing to do with mom not having to cook. Our <u>real</u> reason was because <u>we</u> wanted to go out for pizza.

So we kept on nagging you, and do you know what you did? You broke into a big smile and said, "Sure! Let's all go have pizza!"

You could have bought anything you wanted with your twenty dollars. Candy. Comic books. Some of those play-action figures you liked—the ones you called your "guys."

But instead, you treated your family to a night on the town. What an incredible thing to do. What a wonderful little boy you were!

Anyway, you ended up being the hero of the day. As it turns out, Mom <u>was</u> happy that she didn't have to cook, and we all had a great time at the pizza place. As for Valerie and me, we ended up feeling a little guilty because we knew we'd bullied you into taking everyone to dinner.

But not too guilty to eat the pizza.

Love,

Julie

## julianne moore

Dear Valerie,

The thing I remember most about growing up with you is that I can't remember a day without you. Because I'm only a year and three days older than you, we were very, very close. Mom says that right after you started to learn to walk, she couldn't keep you in your crib. Every time she went in to check on you, she'd discover that you'd escaped. That's when I'd confess to her that I had pulled you out of your crib. Hey, you were my sister. You wanted to get out of the crib? I got you out.

And remember how, when we got a little older, people always thought we were twins, and how we sometimes liked that (and sometimes didn't!)? Sure, we had our differences. Like you were athletic and I wasn't. I liked play-acting, and you didn't. And we did have those fights where we'd wind up drawing a line down the middle of our room. But in the end, we were inseparable. And everyone called us "the girls."

I'll never forget how we used to celebrate birthdays together. And the funniest thing to me was, because we were so close in age and we were both girls, we got everything the same! Well, almost the same. If I got a regular Barbie, you got a Malibu Barbie. If I got a green shirt, you got the same one, only in red. If I got an Easy-Bake oven, you got the Easy-Bake toaster. This became such a custom in our house that when we opened presents, we'd always do it together, remember? Otherwise, whoever was opening her gift second would already know what she was getting.

As we grew older, we still did everything together. Like, whenever we moved to a new city (and that was a lot, right?), we'd always sit together in the school cafeteria. One time we were so scared of our new school, we wouldn't even enter the cafeteria. We sat outside until it got so cold that we had to go in.

And how about that time in high school when I really liked that boy, what's-his-name, but he didn't want to go out with me? Then he told somebody that he really liked you! Remember what you did when you heard that? You walked right up to him and said, "If you don't like my sister, then you don't like me, either." Wow.

So I guess the point of the story is, yeah, we always had the same toys, the same clothes, the same party. But when you stop and think about it, we <u>are</u> the same. And even if we sometimes got tired of being each other's shadow, I never got tired of having you as a friend.

Love,

Julianne

# You Know My Brother
## (He's So Heavy)

Words & music by **Kevin Bacon, Michael Bacon,** and **Robin Batteau**

illustrated by **Loren Long**

You know my brother;
he can be a jerk.
And I gotta cover for him
every time he doesn't do his work.

You know my brother;
he can be a pain.
He's always telling everybody
I'm too dumb to stay out of the rain.

Sometimes it's easy,
sometimes it's rough.
Sometimes I gotta stop him,
sometimes I gotta prop him up.

He's so heavy
when I have to carry him along.
He's so heavy,
but he always seems to make me strong.
You can always find a compromise
when you see it through your brother's eyes.

You know my brother;
he thinks he's so great.
I'm ten minutes early
and my brother is an hour late.

You know my brother;
he thinks he's so cool.
Lightning is striking at random
and he's still in the pool.

Sometimes it's easy,
sometimes it's rough.
Sometimes I gotta stop him,
sometimes I gotta prop him up.

He's so heavy,
but he always seems to make me strong.
He's so heavy—
I mean he's great when we sing a song!
You can always find a compromise
when you see it through your brother's eyes.

I'm so glad we're in this life together.
The more we differ, the more
we're just the same.
When you're a brother, you're a brother forever,
even if he gets all the credit,
and I get all the blame!

You know my brother.
You know my brother. . . .

Sometimes it's easy,
sometimes it's rough.
Sometimes I gotta stop him,
sometimes I gotta prop him up.

He's so heavy—
I mean he's great when we share a song!
He's so heavy,
and he always seems to make me strong!
You can always find a compromise
when you see it through your brother's eyes.

Thank you, my brother.
You know my brother.
Thank you, my brother.

# YOU KNOW MY BROTHER (He's So Heavy)

Words and music by
KEVIN BACON, MICHAEL BACON & ROBIN BATTEAU

# Josie's First Allowance Day

### by ROSIE PEREZ

### illustrated by DAN ANDREASEN

JOSIE WOKE UP with a thrash! Well, it was her birthday week, for goodness' sake! Josie turned seven on Tuesday, and today was Saturday, and Saturday was allowance day—so how *else* would she get out of bed?

In Tia Ana's house, allowances were passed out on Saturdays, and you couldn't get one till you were seven. Well, today Josie was seven and she was going to get her very first allowance! A dollar! That's a whole bunch of money to someone like Josie, thank you very much!

Josie lived with her Tia Ana (that means "Aunt Ana" in Spanish) and her two cousins in New York City's Washington Heights. It was an "island" neighborhood—meaning everyone was from the Caribbean. On Josie's block alone there were people from the Dominican Republic, like Josie and her family, and also people from Puerto Rico, Costa Rica, Haiti, Cuba, St. Croix, St. Thomas, and even Panama, for goodness' sake.

Even though it wasn't like the islands at all—and their apartment was very small and crowded—Josie loved it. She loved how people spoke Spanish and English, just like her. She loved how everyone knew everyone, and how they all looked out for one another. And she loved the way the air was filled with the delicious smells of rice and beans and her favorite, *chuletas* (which are fried pork chops, thank you very much).

On this special Saturday morning, Josie ran over to the shoebox that was her personal office and pulled out her list of things to buy with her allowance. First, of course, was a big, fat, juicy dill-barreled pickle. A person with less sophisticated tastes might have listed something sweet and gooey and chewy first, but not Josie. *That* was her second choice.

Her third choice she left blank. Tia Ana always said there are possibilities in life that you just have to leave open. "Life's best when you go with the flow" (or something like that).

Tia Ana came into Josie's room, dressed for work. "Someone is up very early for a Saturday," she said.

"I was going over my allowance list, Titi Ana," Josie said. "I got three possibilities."

"Well, don't spend it all in one place, Josie," Tia Ana teased. And then she handed Josie a crisp, brand-new dollar bill, and kissed her on the forehead and rubbed it in for good measure. Josie loved it when her aunt did that.

"My own allowance!" yelled Josie. "Oh, how I've waited for this very moment!"

Tia Ana smiled and shook her head. "A Drama Queen, folks. With a capital *D* and a capital *Q*. I'll be back at five," she said, leaving the room. "Love you like a *chuleta.*"

"Love you like *arroz con pollo,*" answered Josie.


JOSIE WAS FIRST in line outside Don Miguel's bodega.

"*Ahola,* Don Miguel!" said Josie as her friend unlocked the gate to his store.

"*Ahola,* Josie, and happy First Allowance Day to you," he replied. "Give me just a minute and I'll let you in."

Josie was at the store extra early to hold a place for her best friend, Angela Terrero. Angela had been getting an allowance since she was five, though it was only fifty cents back then. She always shared her candy with Josie, and now that she got a dollar-fifty, she bought Josie a pickle every Saturday, because that's what best friends do for each other, thank you very much.

"Oh, no," Josie mumbled to herself. "Here comes Stuck-up Carmen and her gang of bullies."

Carmen was the prettiest and most stuck-up girl in the neighborhood. And to make matters disgustingly worse, her family gave her the biggest allowance. Everyone feared Stuck-up Carmen but wanted to be her friend, too—except for Josie and Angela, of course. Secretly, Josie was scared of Carmen, but she never admitted that to anyone, not even to Angela.

"No holding spots allowed, Josie!" shouted Stuck-up Carmen.

"Since when?" asked Josie.

"Since my father spoke to Don Miguel about annoying little pests who hog up the line and don't even have any money. So if you don't have money, you can't be holding no spots!"

It was always surprising to Josie how Stuck-up Carmen spoke. How could anyone with so much money speak so poorly? It just goes to show you that all the money in the world can't buy you class, thank you very much.

"Well, I got my allowance today, so I guess I can stand anywhere I like!" Josie shouted, trembling in her shoes.

"Oh, yeah, prove it!" challenged Stuck-up Carmen.

Josie held out her brand-new dollar bill.

"Wow!" laughed Stuck-up Carmen, as her whole gang of girls joined in the laughter. "A whole dollar! Just think, in four more weeks you could have as much as me!" She waved her five-dollar bill in Josie's face.

"Shut up, Stuck-up Carmen!" blurted Josie, quickly covering her mouth as the words came out. Josie began to shake with fright. She had never had a real fight, let alone one with the prettiest, most stuck-up, and tallest girl in the neighborhood.

Stuck-up Carmen took two steps right up to Josie and said, "I know you didn't just tell me to shut up, you little—!"

"Little what?" roared a voice from behind.

Stuck-up Carmen turned around and found herself face to face with Angela. The gang of girls took a giant step away. Stuck-up Carmen was the prettiest and the richest girl in the neighborhood, but Angela was the toughest, and everyone knew it.

"Let's go to the bodega across the street, girls," said Stuck-up Carmen. "This one is too whack for me."

Josie watched Stuck-up Carmen stomp away with her gang behind her. Then she looked at Angela. "Thanks," she said.

"For what?" asked Angela. "That's what friends do, for goodness' sake. Come on, let's go in."

The girls burst through the door. Josie ran up and down the aisles and then screeched to a stop in front of a display of fake roses, on sale for ninety-nine cents each. Suddenly she started to cry.

"What's wrong?" asked Angela.

Josie choked back the tears. "Well, I only got one dollar," she said. "I was going to buy a pickle for fifty cents, and five ten-cent candies for both of us. But now these fake roses. I feel like I should get one for my Titi Ana. And if I do, I won't have enough to get anything else. I don't know what to do!"

Don Miguel heard the commotion and approached the girls.

"*Qué paso,* Josie?" he asked. "This is a special day for you. You shouldn't be crying!"

"It's just that I want to get my Titi Ana something special . . . ," she began.

"Then how about a beautiful fake rose for ninety-nine cents?" said Don Miguel.

"But then she won't have money for her pickle," stated Angela.

"I don't care about my pickle anymore," cried Josie. "But I can't buy you any candy."

"I can buy my own candy," Angela said, laughing. "And I'll buy you your pickle, too!"

"No," said Josie. "You always look out for me. Today I wanted to look out for you."

"So what? Next week you can look out for me. This week you get your Titi Ana a fake rose and I'll get you a pickle. That's what best friends do for each other, for goodness' sake."

"And I'll throw in some extra ten-cent candy as a first-time allowance prize," added Don Miguel. "*That's* what real neighborhoods are about!"

"You guys are the best friends in the entire universe!" cried Josie.

"Drama Queen!" replied Don Miguel and Angela. *"Dra-ma Queen!"*


JOSIE AND ANGELA sat on their stoop. Josie was devouring her giant pickle and Angela ate more ten-cent candies than you can imagine. Then Stuck-up Carmen passed by, with her gang of girls in tow.

"Wait!" Josie shouted to Carmen, holding out a piece of candy. "No hard feelings?"

Stuck-up Carmen was totally in shock (as she took the candy, of course). "Uh, thank you," she said sheepishly.

"It's nothing," said Josie.

Stuck-up Carmen gave an embarrassed smile, then scurried down the block with her gang of girls.

"I have to go," Josie said to Angela, giving her best friend an extra-big hug. "My Titi Ana will be home soon, and I want to surprise her with her fake rose. What else would a kid do for her loving aunt, for goodness' sake?"

She kissed Angela on the forehead, rubbed it in for extra good measure, and flew up the steps, thank you very much.

# Sing Me the Story of Your Day

words and music by John Forster and Tom Chapin
illustrated by R. Gregory Christie

Sing me the story of your day.
Of the coming and the going,
of another day of growing,
and what you learned along the way.
Sing me the story of your day.

Sing me the story of your day.
A surprising smile that warmed you,
an idea that transformed you.
Show me the game you learned to play.
Sing me the story of your day.

# SING ME THE STORY OF YOUR DAY

Words and music by
JOHN FORSTER & TOM CHAPIN

# AUNT DELIA'S
## HOLIDAY MANNERS
# QUIZ
### (FOR KIDS AND THEIR GROWN-UPS)

**BY DELIA EPHRON**     **ILLUSTRATED BY ED KOREN**

It's time to get ready to go to Thanksgiving dinner. Your aunt and uncle will be there, your grandma and grandpa, your cousins Michelle, Simon, and Matt.
What should you wear?

- Nothing.

- A tutu.

- A clean shirt and pants.

After a long ride in the car, you finally arrive. Your grandma says, "My goodness, look how you've grown."

- Do you say, "And you've shrunk"?

- Do you say, "Thanks"?

- Do you say, "Don't blame me. It's not my fault"?

You mom reminds you to say hello to the baby, your cousin Simon, whom you've never met because he was just born.

- Do you admire him and let him hold your finger in his fist?

- Do you say, "Hi, Baldie, where's your hair"?

- Do you say, "Aunt Delia, don't hold him, hold me!"?

Everyone sits down, and Aunt Delia carries the turkey to the table and gives you your plate. On it she put one creamed onion and it is touching the turkey meat.

- Do you ignore it?

- Do you refuse to eat the turkey because the onion touched it?

- Do you cry?

You eat some cranberry sauce and suddenly realize that it's homemade with little bits of orange rind on top. Oh, no!

- Do you say, "Excuse me, Aunt Delia, but I think there are bird droppings on the cranberry sauce"?
- Do you say, "I hate this kind of cranberry sauce. I like Ocean Spray in a can"?
- Do you leave it on your plate and say nothing?
- Do you pass your plate back and say, "Kindly get this ugly red stuff off my plate"?

Which of these are appropriate subjects for Thanksgiving dinner conversation?

- Whether the turkey knew it was going to die.
- The time cousin Michelle laughed so hard while eating that a hot dog came out of her nose.
- Stink bombs.
- Pilgrims.

You are finished eating before your Uncle Jerry is finished carving.

- Do you sit patiently and wait until everyone else has finished eating?
- Do you disappear under the table and steal napkins from everyone's lap?
- Do you put your head on your plate and go to sleep?

It's time to go home. What's the best way to show everyone how much you love them?

- Give them each a big hug and a kiss and thank Aunt Delia for the delicious dinner.
- Say, "Some Thanksgiving. The only thing I liked was the white meat turkey."
- Say, "So long, Aunt Delia, Uncle Jerry, Grandma, Grandpa, Matt, Michelle, and Baldie. See you at Christmas. Bring big presents."

# Point of View

*by Shel Silverstein*

Thanksgiving dinner's sad and thankless
Christmas dinner's dark and blue
When you stop and try to see it
From the turkey's point of view.

Sunday dinner isn't sunny
Easter feasts are just bad luck
When you see it from the viewpoint
Of a chicken or a duck.

Oh how I once loved tuna salad
Pork and lobsters, lamb chops too
Till I stopped and looked at dinner
From the dinner's point of view.

*Shel Silverstein*

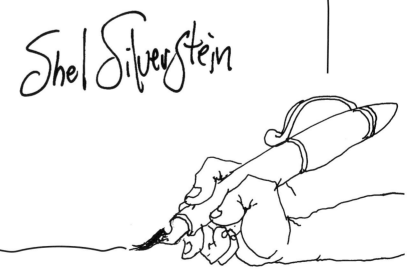

# What Nana Told Her

by Deepak Chopra
illustrated by Demi

Sometimes very good things can come from very sad things. But before I tell you how, you must know two things.

First, my family comes from India. India is a very old country, thousands and thousands of years older than America. It lies so far away that you have to cross three large bodies of water—the Pacific Ocean, the China Sea, and the Indian Ocean—to get to it. I was born and spent my childhood there, and I remember waking each morning to the sound of screechy, brown monkeys and brilliant green parrots fighting over who would get the biggest piece of fruit for breakfast.

When my two children were small, it was exciting for them to return to India, for you see, being born in America, they weren't used to meeting elephants and monkeys and even cobras as an everyday event.

But most of all they were excited to visit their nana. Which brings me to the second thing you need to know. In India, "nana" is what you call your grandfather on your mother's side. In America, "nana" usually means "grandmother," but not in my country so far away.

During one of our family visits to India, my little daughter, Mallika, suddenly stopped finishing all her food at dinnertime. Every evening she would leave behind a piece of bread or some vegetables. I knew she was doing this on purpose, because she would make a neat little pile on the corner of her plate. Then she'd excuse herself and carry her plate, with its small collection of uneaten food, out of the house.

Her mother and I thought this was quite a mystery. After a week we asked her what was going on, and this is the story she told:

Mallika had gone to dinner one night at Nana's house, and she had noticed that everyone in the family left food on their plates. Nobody ate their entire meal, even though the food was very delicious.

"Why do you do that?" she had asked her nana.

"I will tell you because you are old enough to know," Nana replied. "A hundred years ago in one part of India there was a war. Many people were killed or lost everything they had. Our family was among those in danger, and so your ancestors decided to flee.

"One night they packed up and set sail for a safer place to live. But a giant storm came up. It was the middle of the night, and their boat rocked and swayed as if it might sink. The passengers were very scared and wondered if they would have to abandon ship. And that's when a terrible accident happened."

"What?" asked Mallika, seeing her nana grow very sad.

"There were five children before the storm began, but sometime during the night, one was lost at sea and never seen again. To remember that child we leave some food on our plates every evening. Then we go out into the street and give that food to a homeless boy or girl."

Tears came to Mallika's eyes, and she decided that from that moment on she, too, would honor the memory of that child who was lost to our family so long ago. And so, each night at dinner, she had been taking her little bit of food to give to a child who didn't have a home.

To this day, Nana's family observes this wonderful tradition. And that's how a very good thing came from a very sad thing.

EZEKIEL JOHNSON

By Walter Dean Myers
Illustrated by Christopher Myers

Ezekiel Johnson was the kind of big-city character who never makes the newspapers unless he gets into trouble. A tall, gaunt man with enormous hands and a shock of white hair, he could be seen even on the coldest days, pushing around an old shopping cart in which he collected aluminum cans on the street. Ezekiel had set up a cardboard "house" in the fifteen-foot-wide alleyway behind the Acme Theater. He kept the alley clean, so the owners of the theater didn't complain.

But when the Acme was sold and torn down, the new owners wanted to expand the property into a fancy coffee shop with an even fancier Italian name. They decided to use the alleyway to add some outdoor tables, and that's when they found out that Ezekiel Johnson actually owned that small strip of land. A story in the local paper said that they ended up paying seventy-nine-year-old Ezekiel $14,000 for his property.

For a man who was homeless, it was quite a windfall. The local NAACP offered to help Ezekiel invest his newfound dollars, and the neighborhood Baptist Church volunteered to find him a room he could rent. These folks really cared about the old man, so you can imagine how surprised they were when they saw on the evening news that, instead of spending the money on himself, he was donating it all to the homeless shelter over on Maple Avenue so they could buy coats for people who didn't have one.

"Why are you giving your money away?" the TV reporter asked as the camera panned Ezekiel, stopping at the rags he had tied around his legs. "Aren't you homeless?"

"A man ain't just what he owns," Ezekiel answered.

The reporter tried to press Ezekiel for a better answer, but it was clear that the old man wasn't listening. He had already started down the street, pulling his shopping cart behind him.

Ezekiel's story was interesting enough, but it wasn't long before news from the Middle East pushed it out of the headlines, and the world spun away from Ezekiel and his $14,000. The story would probably have been completely forgotten if the next December hadn't been the coldest that anybody could remember.

The TV station assigned a young reporter to do a human-interest

story about the record-low temperatures, and she literally shivered as she interviewed some men huddled around a fire in an open lot.

"Well, the food kitchen down the way is going to be a big help," an old-timer told her. "And we all got good coats from Zeke Johnson. So, cold as it is, it looks like we're going to make it."

The reporter tracked down Ezekiel in time for the late news and asked him how he felt, knowing that his coats were keeping people warm on such a frigid night.

"Don't think much about it," came the slow answer. "If they're keeping warm, then that's good."

"Why did you buy the coats?"

"He that hath two coats, let him impart to him that hath none," Ezekiel said.

"Which means exactly what?" the reporter demanded.

"Means you got to be more than what you own," Ezekiel said.

The reporter couldn't come up with a good response to that, so she decided to reshoot the interview. This time she suggested that Ezekiel must really be proud of himself for making such a useful contribution on a cold night.

"Nothing to be proud about," he replied. "I just did it."

That didn't seem like a good closing line either, so the reporter gave it one last try. This time she ended the interview by saying that *she* was proud of Ezekiel Johnson. Ezekiel just grunted and looked away.

The story ran late, between the traffic and the weather. The TV people tried to make Ezekiel Johnson into a kind of hero, but most folks who saw the interview didn't see him that way. What they saw was an old man, with an odd way of speaking, who was quite a bit more than what he owned.

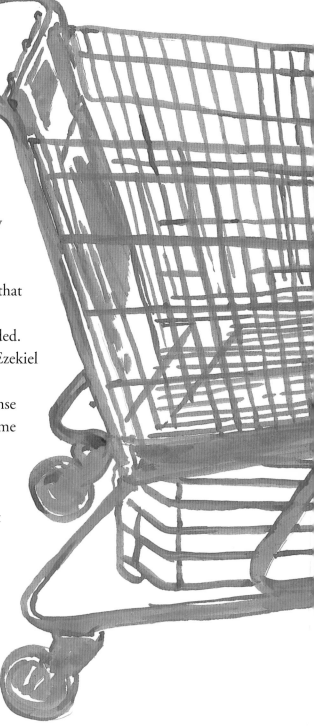

# Geology

## Introduction

### by Paul Newman

My uncle Joe Newman, who was a journalist for the Cleveland Press and who actually taught versification, wrote this poem along with many others, about sixty years ago. But given the way the world turns, or maybe gets stuck on its axis, this one could just as easily have been written this morning.

As my uncle Joe points out, Mother Earth has taken a lot of shots, surviving volcanoes, earthquakes, plate tectonics, ice ages, and what have you. And as if that weren't enough, we humans have chipped in and blown huge holes in her face, clear-cut forests, mucked up the muck under the seas, polluted the air and rivers with every version of miscreant molecule we could devise, and we fight with our siblings as if it is mother love that's at stake.

It's a great privilege to live where and when we do, but that privilege brings some responsibility. The ancient Greeks had it right. They pursued their work up to a given point and then, if they were very fortunate, they focused on giving themselves over to the public service, or working somehow in pursuit of the common good. We could learn a lot from them. At least I have. The big trick is not to do things because they are "important," but to get a good idea and pursue it with a kind of fury. In the final analysis, we will be about as good as people make us. And the places we live will be about as good as we make them.

# Geology

*by Joseph S. Newman*

This ball was once a glowing mass
Of mixed and superheated gas,
Till it cooled to liquid, shrank in girth,
Solidified and turned to earth.
For several thousand endless ages
It muddled through its early stages
Of heat, eruptions, floods, and quakes
And other infant bellyaches.
Surviving all such pains and notions,
It settled down as land and oceans.
In eras that are known as "glacials"
The planet then got several facials—
Four geological massages
In four successive ice barrages—
Which filled its unbecoming dimples
And leveled off some rocky pimples.
If, sometimes, there's a recrudescence,
It's due, no doubt, to adolescence,
But in the main, we now are able
To say the Earth is fairly stable
And, in most geologic features,
Better balanced than its creatures.

*illustrated by David Shannon*

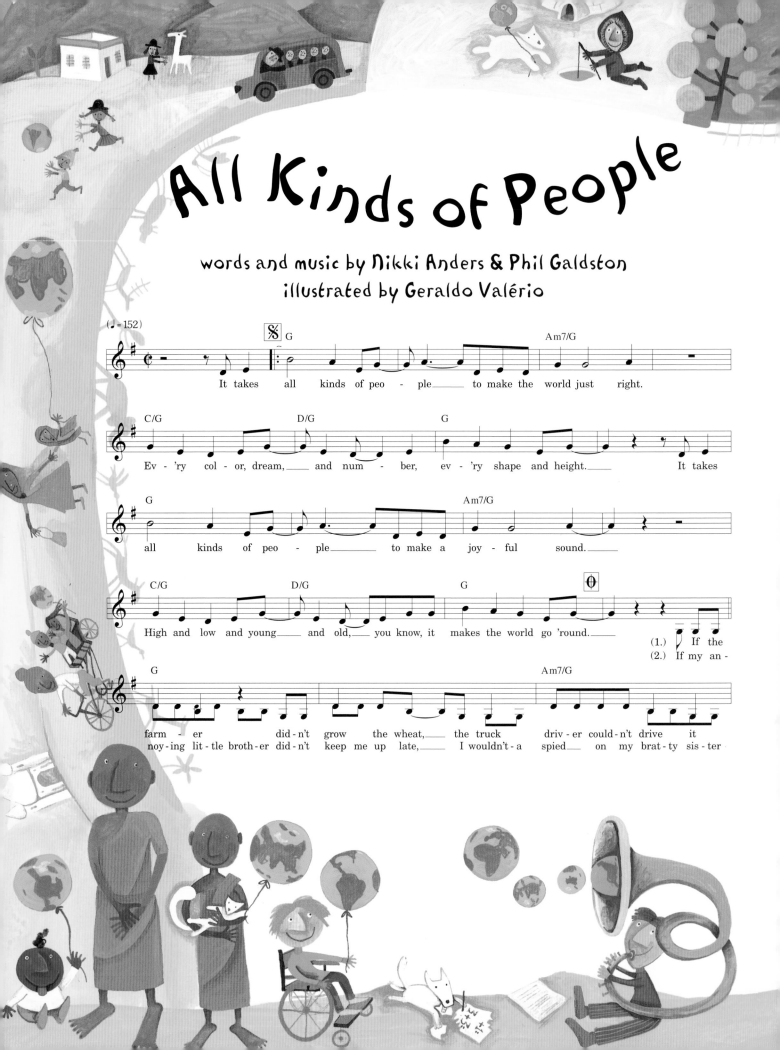

# All Kinds of People

words and music by Nikki Anders & Phil Galdston
illustrated by Geraldo Valério

It takes all kinds of peo - ple to make the world just right.
Ev - 'ry col - or, dream, and num - ber, ev - 'ry shape and height. It takes
all kinds of peo - ple to make a joy - ful sound.
High and low and young and old, you know, it makes the world go 'round.

(1.) If the
(2.) If my an -

farm - er did - n't grow the wheat, the truck driv - er could - n't drive it
noy - ing lit - tle broth - er did - n't keep me up late, I wouldn't - a spied on my brat - ty sis - ter

# what I did with my coin collection

## BY TIGER WOODS          ILLUSTRATED BY SARAH S. BRANNEN

When I was about five, maybe six, years old, I loved to collect coins. I had about a dozen of them, and most special of all were the gold coins—each one big and shiny and sparkling like the sun. My favorite was a twenty-dollar Canadian gold piece.

But if I loved anything in the world more than my coins, it was my own set of golf clubs. My father had made them especially for me. (He took regular grown-up clubs and cut them down to my size.) I kept my clubs in the garage, where Dad had built a big net so I could hit the ball as hard as I wanted to—right into it. He also put in a special green carpet, where I could practice putting.

Was I lucky! Most kids have to drive in a car to play miniature golf. I played *real* golf in my own garage. And not only that—I also golfed with my father almost every day. Here's how I did that: I memorized his telephone number at his office, where he worked for a company that built rockets. That's right—real rockets that carried satellites into space! But that didn't stop me from calling him at his desk every afternoon to ask if I could practice golf with him. My dad was a great golfer— he had a handicap of one. That means he was very good.

"Daddy," I'd say, "are you going to go out and play golf today? Can I go with you? Please?!"

"Oh, I'm not so sure, Tiger," he'd answer. "Maybe today isn't such a good idea."

But then he'd change his mind and say, "Okay, sure." (That's what I always loved about my dad.)

"But you have to finish your homework first," he'd remind me.

And that's exactly what I'd do. In fact, I got so good at doing my homework, I could add, subtract, multiply, and divide at a very young age, and all because I wanted to go play golf with my dad so much.

One night I was watching the news with my father. The man on TV was Walter Cronkite, and he was telling a story about families who lived in Ethiopia, a country in the eastern part of Africa. Their lives were terrible, said Mr. Cronkite. Men and women and boys and girls there were starving to death. Really starving. They had no food at all.

I stared at the TV, more frightened than I'd ever been. The faces of these children were so sad, and flies buzzed around their heads. But it was their eyes that were the scariest of all—big and wide-open and terrified.

I had never even imagined that kids could be this unhappy. I was their age, and I lived in a nice house in California. I had my own room, with my own little TV set. I had a tricycle. I was going to school. And all these kids wanted was just a crust of bread, maybe.

My father saw the look on my face and said, "You know, Tiger, I have a doctor friend who is over in Africa right now, working to help these children."

"That's good," I said, not really feeling much better.

Then my dad quietly explained to me how lucky I was to be living a good and healthy life. He told me that it wasn't the fault of these Ethiopian children that they were starving. He said people all over the world were trying to send food and help to them.

As I listened to my father, I never took my eyes off the TV. Then I got up and went to my room. I stood in the doorway and looked around.

There was my little television. There were my books and my toys. There was my favorite golf club, lying across my bed. And there were my precious coins, the gold Canadian one right on top. The strange thing was, as I looked at all my wonderful stuff, I got very, very sad inside. I kept seeing the faces of those Ethiopian kids. Suddenly the world didn't seem very fair to me, and I knew what I had to do.

I went back into the living room with my box of coins. I gave them to my father, who was still watching TV.

"Daddy," I said, "would you send these to your friend in Africa so he can help those kids and buy some food for them?"

"Are you sure, Tiger?" he asked me. "I know how much you love them."

"I'm sure, Daddy."

My father gave me a hug and said, "Yes, Tiger, I will send them to Africa for you." He took the box of coins from me, and that was that.

For as long as I can remember, we've had a special family saying: "Share and care." Dad tells me that the first time he said those words to me was the day I was born. I don't remember that day, of course, but he and my mother never let a day go by without telling me that we must remember to help others. *Share and care.* I still say those words to myself every day.

By the way, a lot of good things in my life came from those coins. Because I was so interested in Africa as a little boy, I wound up playing golf there when I got older, at a tournament to raise money for people who needed help. And it's also where I got to meet the great leader of South Africa, Nelson Mandela, who helped gain freedom for his people.

Did I ever miss my coins? Sometimes—but that's okay. Because one thing I've learned is that, in the end, sharing and caring is worth a million pieces of gold.

# Nuts to You by Mo Willems

# (I'll Give) Anything but Up

**words and music by HILARY DUFF, SARAH DURKEE, JIM MARR, CHARLIE MIDNIGHT, WENDY PAGE, and MARC SWERSKY**

illustrated by KEN FEISEL

(1.) Here on earth there's so much con-fu-sion. Peo-ple liv-ing in a kind of il-lu-sion that some-bod-y else is mak-ing things bet-ter, but some-how we've got to do it to-geth-er. I am just a true be-liev-er. When it comes to giv-ing, I'm an o-ver-a-chiev-er.

(2.) Some girls are not quite what they seem, a twist-ed lack of self-es-teem. Mir-rors are all they want to see. That's not the way that it should be. Some-times the world is just so small. You can reach an-y-bod-y just by giv-ing your all.

As long as I live, there's more I can give. It's nev-er e-nough. I'll give an-y-thing but up. As far as I go, there's one thing I know. It's nev-er too tough, oh no, I'll give an-y-thing but up.

# THE NOTHINGEST GIRL IN THE WORLD

by BRUCE KLUGER  illustrated by HENRY COLE

She had nothing at all,
  nothing fancy or fine
    like Penelope's gown with
      the tulip design.

    Like Natalie's dollhouse,
      like Cynthia's hats,
      like Lacey's spectacular
        Siamese cats.

      Whenever they gathered,
    the girls would all boast,
and practically worship the one who
    had most.

And that's when Delilah would turn
    a shade red,
and hear those same words
    spinning 'round in her head:

  *"I'm just plain Delilah!
  Old worthless Delilah!
  The nothingest girl in the
    world."*

It happened one Friday when school was
    on break,
at Jessie's big birthday event by the lake.

As always, the girls couldn't wait to display
the presents they'd brought to give
    Jessie that day.

Teresa gave Twister, Melinda gave art,
and Gwen gave a locket the shape of a heart.

And Sara gave powder
    (the kind with a puff),
and Lulu gave all sorts of
    roller-skate stuff.

"Oh, no!" thought Delilah
    in total defeat.
"There's simply no way I can hope to compete."

Instead of a gift, she had worked really hard
on something as dumb as a hand-painted card.

"How stupid!" she groaned as she tossed
    it aside,
    then sat by the lake with an ache
      in her pride.

    So thoroughly saddened,
      so wholly resigned,
      she heard those old words
      bubble up in her mind:

    *"I'm just plain Delilah!
    Old worthless Delilah!
    The nothingest girl in the world."*

Though doomy and gloomy and bluer
    than blue,
Delilah knew just what she needed
    to do:

Whenever she found herself
    anxious or sad,
or reeling from anger, or feeling
    just bad.

Or hurting from something
     that somebody said,
mysterious music would
     play in her head.

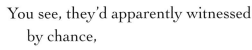

Then, body in motion,
     and head in a trance,
Delilah would joyously
     break into dance.

And always, but always, in just a short while,
the frown on her face would ignite as a smile.

And that is precisely what happened this day,
with all of her friends just a few feet away.

She kicked and she leapt and she buzzed
     and she whirred;
and she spun like a top and she soared
     like a bird.

She danced till her sorrow was nowhere
     about.
And that's when she heard her friend
     Monica shout:

"Is that really you? Are my eyes playing
     tricks?
Those twirlies and whirlies! Those
     high-stepping kicks?!"

And just as Delilah turned 'round
     to reply,
a glorious spectacle greeted her eye:

All of them—all of them!—standing aside,
their jaws fairly dropping, their eyes opened
     wide.

You see, they'd apparently witnessed
     by chance,
     Delilah's delightful, delirious
     dance!

     "Again!" shouted Rosie.
"Once more!" hollered Ling.
And Carly (for once) couldn't
     utter a thing.

Then Jessie stepped up to Delilah with glee.
"Well, *that*," she said warmly, "was something
     to see!

"You move like an angel, so graceful
     and swift.
Your dancing, Delilah, is surely
     a *gift*."

"A gift?" thought Delilah. "So that's
     how it goes!
A gift doesn't need to have ribbons
     or bows.

"It needn't be ritzy or swanky or smart.
*A gift can be something that comes from the heart!*"

And that, for Delilah, was how the day ended:
     by feeling so newly (and *truly*) befriended.

     And later that night when she lay in her
     bed,
     a new kind of thought buzzed around in her
     head:

     *"I'm truly Delilah!*
     *Uniquely Delilah!*
     *The somethingest girl in the world."*

# Right Under *your* Nose

by MEL BROOKS

illustrated by Paul O. Zelinsky

Oh, boy, am I in trouble! My fifth-grade American history final is set for tomorrow morning at ten o'clock and I know for sure I'm going to flunk, and then I'll have to face a ten-year-old Brooklyn boy's worst nightmare: SUMMER SCHOOL!

Why am I so certain I'm going to flunk? Because my fifth-grade teacher, Mrs. Simon, told us exactly what the test will consist of: We'll be asked to list the names of at least thirty of the fifty-nine signers of the Declaration of Independence. I know some of them right off the top of my head, of course, like Benjamin Franklin. But even though the names of all fifty-nine are listed in the back of my history book, they all seem to jumble in my mind into a confusing blur.

Frankly, I'm pretty smart in school, a whiz in arithmetic and a darn good speller. But memorizing long lists of names has definitely never been my strong suit.

It's late on a spring evening, almost midnight, and I'm sitting alone at the kitchen table in our fifth-floor walk-up tenement apartment at 365 South 3rd Street near Hooper Street in long-ago Brooklyn, New York,

U.S.A. By this time of night, I should've long since been reading a Dick Tracy comic book with a flashlight under the covers of my bed. But instead I am staying up hour after hour, trying hopelessly to remember all those early-American names, none of which sound to me like *real* last names—like the names of our neighbors, the Moskowitzes, the Steinbergs, the Cohens, and the Levinsons.

My mother and two of my three older brothers, Lenny and Bernie, have long since gone to bed, but now, as midnight strikes, I hear a key in the door. In comes my oldest brother, Irving, who is twenty and is going to Brooklyn College at night while working full-time during the day as a shipping clerk in hopes of keeping our family financially afloat.

My father died when I was only two years old, so I've grown up with Irving as a surrogate father—he's been my role model, my mentor, my hero. "All four of us brothers," I remember Irving telling me, "we're smart and we're going to get an education, go to college even! We're going to *read* our way out of poverty!"

I always turn to Irving whenever I have troubles, and now I have tears streaming down my cheeks when I tell him all about my failed attempt to memorize the names of the signers.

"You can't remember them, huh?" says Irving with a gleam in his eye that suggests that he knows something I don't. "Well, I think I know exactly why Mrs. Simon decided to test you on the names of the signers. And I'm going to tell you why. But first, let me see if you can answer a few simple questions."

"Like what?" I say, slightly confused.

"Like, where do you and the rest of the guys play stickball every afternoon?"

"That's easy," I reply. "Over on Rutledge Street."

"Right!" says Irving. "Next question. Where is Herstein's drugstore?"

"That's easy, too," I say. "Herstein's is on Hooper Street."

"Right again!" says Irving. "And where's your school?"

"Every kid knows where his school is, Irv," I say. "It's at the corner of South 1st and Rodney."

"Correct!" says Irving. "Now one final question: What's the name of the section of Brooklyn that we live in?"

"C'mon, that's the easiest one of all," I say. "We live in Williamsburg!"

"Of course we do," says Irving. "And why is it called Williamsburg? Because it's named after Williamsburg, Virginia, where men like Thomas Jefferson and George Wythe first dreamed up the idea of writing a Declaration of Independence—and later signed it. Now do you get it?"

"Get what?" I say, still confused.

"Get that when the city fathers laid out Williamsburg, Brooklyn," says Irving, "they named practically all of the streets in honor of the signers of the Declaration of Independence! Look at your list of signers. They're the same names as the streets all around us—Rutledge and Hooper and Rodney, Whipple and Hewes and Clymer."

A lightbulb comes on over my head!

"Then I don't have to memorize them!" I shout and give a loud whoop of joy. "Because I already know them! I walk on all those guys, I play on all those guys!

"You sure do!" says Irving, as he gives me a big good-night hug and sends me happily off to bed.

And guess what? The next day I ace that American history test! Final mark for little Melvin: 100! Final payoff for little Melvin: NO SUMMER SCHOOL! Thank you, Irving!

And what is the moral of my little story of long ago in Williamsburg, Brooklyn, U.S.A.? I think maybe there are two.

One: If you're a little kid and you're having trouble with something like homework, it is perfectly okay to ask for help from someone older than you, like your parents or a big brother, as long as you ask them only for guidance and not actually to do your homework for you.

And two: Lots of times the answers to problems that seem impossible to solve are staring you in the face. They are, in short, RIGHT UNDER YOUR NOSE!

# The Rotten Tomato

## (Based on a True Story)
## (Actually, Really a True Story)

### by WENDY WASSERSTEIN

The action takes place in the bedroom of Lucy Jane, who is four-going-on-five years old. It is 8:30 p.m. Lucy Jane should have been asleep an hour ago. She sits upright on her bed, wide awake. Her mother sits next to her, tired but attentive.

**LUCY JANE:** Mommy, tell me another story. Tell me the one about the rotten tomato.

**MOMMY:** Okay. But let's make it a story about the nice tomato.

**LUCY JANE:** There can be a nice tomato, but I want a rotten tomato, too. And the rotten tomato has to win.

**MOMMY:** In my house, the *nice* tomato has to win.

**LUCY JANE:** No. The rotten tomato.

**MOMMY:** Okay. Then maybe there can be some other vegetables that are nice. There can be a nice carrot, and a nice pepper, and a nice cucumber . . .

**LUCY JANE:** Fine. But the rotten tomato has to win.

**MOMMY:** Have it your way. But remember, nobody *likes* the rotten tomato. The rotten tomato doesn't have any friends.

**LUCY JANE:** Why not?

**MOMMY:** Because he's rotten.

**LUCY JANE:** Well, this rotten tomato has *lots* of friends.

**MOMMY:** Maybe. But they're only his friends because they're too scared not to be.

**LUCY JANE:** Does the nice tomato have friends?

**MOMMY:** Oh, yes. The nice tomato has *lots* of friends.

**LUCY JANE:** How come?

**MOMMY:** Because the nice tomato knows how to share, and to be a good friend to others. In fact, all of the other vegetables—the carrots, the peppers, the cucumbers— always want to hang out with the nice tomato. And you know what? When the nice tomato takes on the rotten tomato—which always seems to happen—all the nice vegetables gather round the nice tomato and say to him, "We want to help *you*."

*[Note to grown-ups: This goes on every night. I swear to God.]*

**LUCY JANE** *(concerned):* Fine. But what happens to the rotten tomato?

**MOMMY:** The rotten tomato sees that the nice tomato has all of these friends who are *real* friends. And, of course, the rotten tomato realizes that it's better to be a nice tomato than a rotten tomato.

**LUCY JANE:** So then?

**MOMMY:** So then he tries very hard to be generous and kind and caring. But all of the other vegetables don't believe it. They're not sure he can pull it off.

**LUCY JANE:** Can he?

**MOMMY:** Yes, he can. And he does! One day the rotten tomato realizes that even he can change.

**LUCY JANE:** And?

**MOMMY:** And he becomes a nice tomato.

**LUCY JANE:** Okay, Mom. I understand. *(Pause.)* Now can you tell me a story about a rotten banana?

Tomato illustrated by
Lucy Jane Wasserstein, age 4

58

# WHAT RUBY SAW

by AVI

illustrated by JERRY PINKNEY

Ruby—ten years old—and her father were vacationing on Nantucket Island, staying at a seaside inn for two weeks. It was just the two of them. "You're growing up so fast," her father explained. "This may be the last time I can spend time with my little girl."

They took walks, had picnics, read books. They went swimming and fishing, went looking for shells. Ruby even took boat-rowing lessons from Mr. Cartwright, the old fisherman who worked at the wharf.

Two nights before going home Ruby's father tucked her into bed.

"Are mermaids real?" Ruby asked. She had been reading a book about mermaids and loved how free they were beneath the sea.

Her father laughed and gently touched the tip of her nose. "You're a mermaid," he said.

Ruby knew she wasn't a mermaid. Mermaids always had long hair. She had short, dark, and curly hair. "Dad," she said, "I really want to know what you think."

Her father smiled. "I'm afraid I don't believe in mermaids."

"Is that," asked Ruby, "because you never saw one?"

"Except in stories," her father said, "I'm afraid no one has seen one."

"I don't think they like to be seen," said Ruby. "They live in the mist. And do you know what? They disguise themselves. You have to have special eyes to see them."

"A child's eyes," her father replied with a smile. "But a big girl like you needs to be looking for real things."

Ruby frowned. "You think I'm too old to see mermaids, don't you?"

"Ruby," her father replied, "when we get older, we put aside old dreams. We look for new ones."

"Then I'm not sure I want to grow up."

Her father laughed again. "I'm afraid you don't have a choice." He gazed into Ruby's eyes, then gave her a soft kiss on the cheek and said—as he or Ruby's mom always did at night—"Sweet dreams!" This time he added, "My big girl."

Ruby—as she did every night—asked, "What should I dream about?" She loved the idea of sharing dreams with her parents.

"Mermaids," her father suggested. "Dream about them one last time."

As her father left the room, Ruby thought, *What's the point of getting older if you're not allowed to see mermaids?* Dreaming about them wasn't good enough. She wanted to see a real one. Mermaids seemed so free, the way Ruby wanted to be. Is that what her father was saying, that she mustn't dream about being free?

*All right,* Ruby thought, *I'll look for one by myself.* She set her alarm clock for five o'clock in the morning.

At a little after five in the morning Ruby was on the wharf, which stood just below their inn. A thick gray mist filled the air. It hid the inn behind her. It hid the sky. It hid the bay before her and the ocean beyond. It was as if Ruby had gone to sleep in one world and had woken up in another. *Perfect for mermaids,* she thought.

She listened intently. There was the tinkle of a buoy bell in the bay, the gentle sounds of water washing against the wooden wharf—like a cat lapping milk—the squawk of gulls somewhere overhead hidden by the mist.

At the end of the wharf a number of small boats were tied. "Dinghies," Mr. Cartwright had called them. People used them when they moored big boats in the bay and wanted to come to land. They were perfect for her size, and Ruby had learned to row in one of them.

She climbed down a small wooden ladder, reached out, and pulled a boat close. It was creamy white, trimmed with varnished wood about its gunnels. Two small oars were tucked neatly under the middle seat.

Ruby stepped into the boat. She steadied herself, then drew out the oars and set them in the oarlocks. It was easy to untie the rope and push off.

The boat floated free. Ruby settled herself in the middle of the center seat as Mr. Cartwright had taught her, and began to row.

She rowed with her back toward the direction she wanted to go. But even if Ruby had looked, the mist was so dense she would have seen little beyond the water around the boat.

After fifteen strokes she paused and gazed around. Her dinghy was an island surrounded by a bit of sea and a universe of mist. Uneasy, Ruby started to stand, as if by being taller she might see something. Her shifting weight caused the boat to rock ominously. She sat down quickly.

She listened and heard the same sounds as before: the buoy, quite remote, waves flapping against the boat, and now and again the lonely screech of a gull. Ruby stared into the swirling mist and tried not to be frightened.

Certain of the direction of the wharf, Ruby began to row. After twenty strokes, each one harder than the last, each one a little more desperate, she stopped. The boat drifted. No wharf was in sight. Worse, it felt as if she had not moved at all, but was in exactly the same place she'd been before.

"Hello!" Ruby shouted.

No answer.

She shouted three more times, louder each time. No one replied. *The world is asleep,* she told herself. *Except me. I should stay where I am,* she told herself. *The mist will go. I'll see where I am, then row back to the wharf.*

Ruby waited, watched, and listened. A lot of time seemed to pass. Nothing happened. Was the boat drifting or not? *Maybe I'll drift out to sea. If so I'll be lost forever.* She wanted to cry but pushed the sobs down, even as she wiped away the tears. *Be patient,* she told herself.

"I wish I hadn't come," she said out loud. Then, with a catch in her voice, she whispered, "I wish I hadn't believed in mermaids."

No sooner had she spoken that last sentence than she heard something. She wasn't sure what it was. It sounded like a wave washing against the beach. The idea made her heart leap with joy. Had she drifted toward land? The sound came twice, and then ceased.

Ruby stared at the spot where she thought the sound had come from. It came again—on the other side.

She swiveled quickly. It was the same wavelike sound. And something else. A sound that made Ruby think of a snort. Or perhaps someone . . . breathing.

Ruby held her breath. The breathing sound came again, closer. From a different place. It was as if something—whatever it was—was circling her.

She thought of sharks. Didn't they circle?

Ruby, looking first one way, then another, gripped the boat oars tightly. Her heart was beating furiously.

In the water, off to the right, bubbles frothed on the surface. Alarmed, Ruby stared at them. The next moment, two black eyes were staring at her. Just as she realized that they were eyes, they disappeared below the water.

Ruby gasped. A mermaid. It had to be.

"I'm dreaming," she said out loud and even pinched herself. She didn't waken. She was still in the boat on the water. Still surrounded by mist. But suddenly, the eyes were staring at her again.

That time Ruby saw more of the face. It was a glistening blue-black creature with a long snout, a black nose, and whiskers.

"A seal," cried Ruby.

The seal had been on her left side. Now, with a roll of water, it was on the right. It even rose up partially above the water's surface, as if trying to get a better look at her.

The two stared at one another.

"Are you a mermaid in disguise?" asked Ruby. "If you are—and you can take me home—I'll promise never to give away your disguise."

The seal cocked its head, then plunged beneath the water. Ruby's heart seemed to sink with it. But a few yards away the seal burst up again. It looked back at Ruby.

"She understood me," Ruby whispered. She began to row after the seal.

The seal, never so far away as to become lost in the mist, kept rising and falling upon the water's surface, like a needle stitching a hem. Ruby followed, rowing as hard as she could. "Not so fast!" she called one time.

The seal slowed.

Ten minutes later Ruby saw the wharf in the thinning mist. Tears came again but this time from relief.

She stood up. The seal had swum off but paused to look at her. "Thank you, Mermaid," Ruby called. "I'll keep your secret forever."

The seal barked one short bark, then rolled beneath the water.

When Ruby rushed into the dining room of the inn, her father was already eating his breakfast. "There you are!" he called. "Where have you been? Looking for shells for mom?"

"Looking for mermaids," Ruby said as she sat down. She was feeling very hungry.

When her father said, "Oh, did you see one?" Ruby said, "Only a seal."

"Ah," said her father, with a smile, "You have grown up."

Ruby looked at him. Being older, she suddenly realized, was remembering you were young—but not telling.

# You Made My Day

words and music by **SHELDON HARNICK**      illustrated by **ERIC CARLE**

Con - sid - er - ing the things I've been see - ing, it's a-

maz - ing that such or - di - nar - y sights, such plain and sim - ple sights, can

fill me with a sense of well - be - ing.

(1.) I see a sprink - ler wa - ter - ing a lawn,
(2.) Is that a paint - box float - ing on the breeze?

mak - ing a per - fect rain - bow in the wa - ter-drops.
No, it's a ver - y or - di - nar - y but - ter - fly.

I watch the sun set. Soon it will be gone,
A streak of scar - let flash - es through the trees.

# Thanking Is Just One Letter Away from Thinking

## by Larry Gelbart        illustrated by Karen Katz

"Not too much water, Melody," her mother said.

Her parents had named her Melody because, from the moment she was born, they knew that she would be the music of their lives.

Like all music, Melody could sometimes be too noisy. She could sometimes be too loud. Sometimes she could go on and on and on, long after she should have stopped. None of that ever mattered, though. To her mom and dad, Melody would always be their very favorite song.

"Just enough so that the seeds won't be thirsty," her mother, who was very good at adding, added.

"When I was a seed, did you have to put me in the dirt and water me?" Melody asked.

Melody's mother would often tell people what a wonderful imagination her little daughter had. Being so young, Melody couldn't even imagine what imagination meant. But imagine she did, even if she didn't know that there was a special word for what she was doing.

Though her mother explained that people were different from flowers, Melody wondered if the flowers knew that. Maybe they couldn't think when they were just little seeds, but they'd probably be able to think once they grew all the way up through the dirt and started to have faces.

That night, after the seeds had been sown and watered and tucked into their flower bed—and after Melody had been soaped and watered and tucked into her own—Melody's father read her a story. It was something that Melody would one day do with her own little children, telling them just exactly what her father had always told her: that every story was a ticket to a dream.

After he had finished reading and had given his daughter a kiss to sleep on, Melody's father turned out the lamp beside her bed and quietly left the room. Melody knew that her big, strong father would be able to protect her from anything. Knowing that he could make it seem as though he were almost as little as she was also made her feel just as safe, even if it was in a different kind of way.

Alone and not the least bit sleepy, Melody went to her window so that she could look down at the backyard, down at the spot in which her flower seeds slept. Or were they as wide awake as she was? She tried hard to imagine what they were thinking, if they were still up, and what they might be dreaming, if they were asleep.

She wondered, too, if the big old tree that stood next to the flower bed knew that there were some brand-new seeds sleeping almost at the foot of its trunk? That pretty soon the tree would have a bright ring of color where now there was only a ring of dirt?

The thing about wondering is that one wonder always leads to another—and so Melody started wondering if the old car tire tied to the old tree that she used for a swing had things going around and around inside its own mind too?

Did the tire ever get as dizzy as Melody did when her father pushed her so high up into the air that she could see the bird's nest on the branch of the tree, the one with the three little eggs inside it?

And did the worms that the mother bird would soon be digging up around the old tree to feed her tiny chicks, did they all have their own wormy thoughts too?

Then, because her head was getting so crowded with so many wonderings, Melody decided to get back into her bed.

The very last thought she had before her eyes turned their lights out was that, just in case all of the things she shared her world with *could* think—*could* have thoughts just the way she could—she would never do anything that might hurt them.

She would always make them feel as safe as she could—just the way her mother and father always made her feel.

And even if they didn't understand that, she did. And that made her feel warm inside. That made her feel good. That made her feel thankful. Thankful for herself. And thankful for all the things in this world.

# "Thank you, Mrs. Abruzzi"

## by Ray Romano
## illustrated by Lisa Kopelke

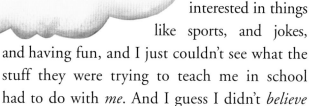

When I was a kid, my father told me over and over again how important it was for me to get a good education. "Knowledge is power!" he would bellow. Whenever we talked about school or college, he'd scream it: "Knowledge is power!"

Then he found out how much a college education costs. "On the other hand," he decided, "what you don't know won't hurt you!"

As I moved through my school years, it became clear that—considering how poorly I was doing in class—he probably wasn't going to have to *worry* about finding enough money to send me to college. Having to pay my room and board for the rest of his life seemed a more likely possibility.

I *did* somehow manage to make it through elementary school—with *very* average grades. But it was in high school that my talent for failing truly showed itself.

I flunked out of the first two schools I went to. It wasn't that I had a hard time learning stuff. It was that I had a hard time *wanting*

to learn. I was interested in things like sports, and jokes, and having fun, and I just couldn't see what the stuff they were trying to teach me in school had to do with *me*. And I guess I didn't *believe* that I was truly very good at anything.

What made things the hardest was that both of my brothers did absolutely fine in school. That was really annoying. You may have noticed that brothers like to rub in your face things that they do better than you. Of course, as we get older, we grow out of such foolishness. (Well, maybe I didn't *entirely* grow out of it. Every once in a while, I send them a copy of one of my TV paychecks along with a note saying "Gotcha!" But I'm getting ahead of my story. . . .)

The *third* school I attended after I left grammar school was a public high school called Hillcrest. It was in Queens, which is part of New York City, and it was supposed to be a little easier than all the schools that I had gone to so far. They told me I could graduate if I could just manage to get passing grades during my final year there. The idea that I could flunk out of two schools and still graduate on time, without having to be "left back," sounded great.

Besides, Hillcrest let you choose all your own courses. You could pick any subject that interested you. Right away, I decided to take six gym classes. They told me I couldn't do that.

I ended up with *one* gym class and, among other things, my first creative writing class. My writing teacher was named Mrs. Abruzzi.

On the first day of school Mrs. Abruzzi asked us to write a short story. Maybe she guessed we weren't used to succeeding, because she gave us the first sentence as a head start. Our job was to take that sentence and continue the story from there. The first sentence she wrote was this: "On the day my grandmother died, I couldn't stop crying."

I looked at that sentence for a long time, and I didn't have a clue where to go with it. I tried for a while to write something really sad and dramatic, but the words just kind of lay there on the page.

Then I thought of something completely different. . . . Let's go *funny*! My second sentence described Grandma's tragic passing, which involved something about a bet she made with my grandpa in a

bar, and a very large burrito. I'm not sure, as I think back on it, how funny the whole story really was. But, at the time, it made me laugh like crazy.

I handed it in with the dread that maybe Mrs. Abruzzi would freak, and that I'd fail once again. But . . . Mrs. Abruzzi *liked* it! She wrote that it was "inventive" and "ingenious" and some other words that I didn't quite understand except to know that she didn't think my story stunk.

On that day, I discovered a feeling that was new and entirely unexpected. It was hope.

Now, I'm not going to tell you everything was great after that. But I did manage to make it through the year, all the way to graduation. Mrs. Abruzzi had shown me that there was actually something I could be good at. And as I continued to write, I somehow discovered my true voice in comedy.

Everything worked itself out. I found a career—something that I truly wanted to do with my life. And my father saved a fortune on room and board.

The one thing I'm sorry about is that I never went back and thanked Mrs. Abruzzi. Her gift was that she encouraged the good in people, no matter how hard it was to find, and for that I will always be grateful.

Well, better late than never. Thank you, Mrs. Abruzzi!

# UNSUNG HEROES

BY CHRISTOPHER CERF AND NORMAN STILES
ILLUSTRATED BY TOM LICHTENHELD

We love to say "I love you" to the folks we're mad about,
But forget to thank the objects that we just can't do without.
It's time we paid them back for all the things they help us do. . . .
So, you small but useful things, I wrote this song for you!

My heart goes out to zippers, buttons, snappers, knots, and bows,
If it weren't for you, I'd freeze because I couldn't close my clothes.
And I couldn't take home things I buy without you, paper sack,
So I offer you my love, although you cannot love me back.

Thank you, plugs and stoppers—you hold water in our sinks.
And without you, corks and bottle caps, we'd surely spill our drinks.
Let's raise a cup to cups, and to the handles used to raise you.
I know you cannot hear me; still I'll sing this song to praise you.

If it weren't for you, galoshes, when it snowed I'd have cold toes,
And if I didn't have my hanky, well, I couldn't blow my nose
(Unless, of course, I blew it on my collar or my cuff),
So though you can't say "You're welcome," I can't thank you both enough.

I pledge my love to lightbulbs, 'cause you help us light our planet,
And you stones who hold my beach towel down, I won't take you for granite!
Yes, thanks to all you things for all the things that you things do. . . .
You are truly unsung heroes, and I sung this song for you!

# Snow, Aldo

by *Kate DiCamillo*        illustrated by *Harry Bliss*

Once, I was in New York,
in Central Park, and I saw
an old man in a black overcoat walking
a black dog. This was springtime
and the trees were still
bare and the sky was
gray and low and it began, suddenly,
to snow:
big fat flakes
that twirled and landed on the
black of the man's overcoat and
the black dog's fur. The dog
lifted his face and stared
up at the sky. The man looked
up, too. "Snow, Aldo," he said to the dog,
"snow." And he laughed.
The dog looked
at him and wagged his tail.

If I was in charge of making
snow globes, this is what I would put inside:
the old man in the black overcoat,
the black dog,
two friends with their faces turned up to the sky
as if they were receiving a blessing,
as if they were being blessed together
by something
as simple as snow
in March.

# Christmas
## and my
# Magic Mom

### by *Whoopi Goldberg*
### illustrated by *Elise Primavera*

hen I was a little girl, my mother worked magic. I'm sure of this now, but at the time, I could never figure it out.

I was about five or six years old, living in a small apartment in the Chelsea area of New York City. It was just my mother, my older brother, and me.

We didn't have a lot of money, but we had each other. I remember every year about a week before Christmas, the magic would begin: A tree would suddenly appear in our living room. Just a naked tree—no decorations, no explanations.

No one would ever mention where the tree came from, or how it got into our living room. And yet my brother and I knew it couldn't have come from my mom. After all, we were always together and we never saw her go out and buy a tree.

"Where did it come from?" I would say to my big brother, Clyde, as we stood side by side in our living room staring at it. "It's almost like it just . . . fell from the sky."

But the magic didn't stop there. The morning after the tree arrived, the first thing we'd do is run into the living room, and there would be lights on the branches. And tinsel. And sprayed snow and Christmas balls and lights that bubbled.

By now we were watching our mother like a hawk—but we never saw her touch that tree.

It *had* to be magic.

Every day leading up to Christmas was just like that. We'd wake up and the tree would be decorated some more. Meanwhile, the living room windows were getting in on the act. They gradually became decorated with pink stenciled snowflakes that looked like they'd been made with that cleaning spray stuff from the kitchen.

Around this time my brother and I would start thinking about our presents. We knew they were coming, of course, so before the big day, we would look everywhere for them. Our apartment wasn't what you'd call big, so it didn't take us long to search everywhere—in the closets, in the bathroom, under our beds.

Nothing.

Finally, Christmas day would arrive, and my brother and I would get up while it was still dark outside. Some years, it would be snowing outside. We'd run into the living room and stop dead in our tracks. The sight was amazing. There was a bicycle. A Flexible Flyer sled. A Lionel train set. A Kate Greenaway dress for me, a Robert Hall suit for my brother. How did she do it?

Where had all this stuff been hiding? At the neighbors'? Under the floorboards? Or maybe Mom had secretly been corresponding with the North Pole all along. You know, talking to Claus.

After we opened our Christmas presents, we'd give our mother hers. We usually made things for her. She always seemed to love our homemade presents as much as we loved the ones we'd gotten.

Anyway, we never really had any time to think about it—we had to get outside! Usually there were about forty-five tons of snow on the streets. So we'd get all dressed up in our snow clothes and head outdoors. My brother would take me onto Tenth Avenue, which by this time would be closed on account of the snow. He'd put me on the front of the Flexible Flyer, then he'd sort of run and pull me along. We'd have the best time.

At first you could see nothing but clean, white snow all around you. Soon the streets would start to fill up—not with cabs and buses like usual, but with kids and their parents. So much for the clean, white snow!

Still, as much fun as we had sledding—and as wonderful as those presents were—the best present for me is the memory of it all. I can still see every moment in my head. That was Mom's real magic.

By the way, when my brother and I got older, we finally asked our mother where the tree and all those presents came from. In fact, we *still* ask her. You know what she says?

"I don't know what you're talking about."

After all these years, Mom still won't give it up.

# PRESENTS I HAVE KNOWN

by **Frankie Muniz**              illustrated by **David Catrow**

**STUPIDEST PRESENT I EVER GOT:** One birthday all I wanted was a red wagon, just like any other three-year-old. Only problem: I was fourteen at the time. I thought it would be cool to put stuff in it and pull it around behind my bike. Wrong. You shoulda heard my friends. "Yo, dude, what's up with the red wagon?" Talk about embarrassing.

**COOLEST GIFT I EVER GOT—LITERALLY:** My mom once got me a Sno-Kone machine. Not the little plastic one with Snoopy on the front (I already had that), but the real deal—the kind you see at carnivals. I started cranking out Sno-Kones right away. I can't remember how many I ate, but I do know it took three days for my mouth to thaw out.

**MOST SHOCKING GIFT—LITERALLY:** A trick pen that shocks you when you click it. A fan sent it to me in the mail—but I got the last laugh. A nosy friend of mine was over when I opened it. He grabbed the pen from me and pushed in the button at the top. He musta jumped fifty feet. Guess that taught him not to touch my stuff.

**MOST ANNOYING PRESENT I ALWAYS GOT:** Clothes, clothes, and more clothes. Worst ever? A brown V-neck sweater. Sometimes I wouldn't even open them (you can tell from the box that they're clothes). Mom would say, "You forgot this one, Frankie." I'd say, "Gee, I guess I overlooked it. . . ." What was I really thinking? *Where are the toys? Bring on the toys!*

**BIGGEST CHRISTMAS-PRESENT BUMMER:** Broken stuff—which happens to me all the time, usually before I even get the gift out of the box. The only thing that ever works is the toothbrush they stick in my stocking every year. And it isn't even electric.

**THE ONE GIFT I WISH I COULD GIVE TO HUMANKIND:**

The love of family, the joy of friendship, and everlasting peace on earth. After that, I think everybody on the planet should have a Sno-Kone machine. The world would be a much happier place.

# CHEESYBREADVILLE

by Sonia Manzano
illustrated by Jon J Muth

In old Puerto Rico, a long time ago,
There lived a poor farmer they called Señor Joe.

Now, Joe was so poor he had little to eat—
To him, even moldy old cheese was a treat!

So one holiday eve—with not much else to give—
He wrapped up some cheese for his wife, Doña Viv.

He'd just tied the bow on the big cheesy ball,
When he heard his wife's footsteps outside in the hall.

As she entered the kitchen, Joe, taken aback,
Hid his gift—just in time!—'neath the oven's third rack.

Joe sighed with relief, then he hugged Viv and said,
"*¡Qué sueño!*—I'm sleepy! I'm going to bed!"

Well, the moment he left, Viv broke into
   a grin;
Then she pulled from the cupboard a
   rusty old tin.

Inside was some cornmeal
   she'd planned, far ahead,
To use to bake Joe a surprise
   loaf of bread.

Doña Viv was excited; her
   timing was right!
She could let the bread bake
   in the oven all night!

Which she did, 'cause she
   wasn't the least bit aware
That the cheese wrapped in
   paper was also in there.

Viv and Joe slept like logs, but awoke the next morn
To the stink of burnt paper, burnt cheese, and burnt corn!

They ran toward the kitchen and, as you can guess,
When they got there they screamed, "What a horrible mess!"

The cheese was on fire, the bread belching smoke—
What an unkindly sight for these kindly old folk!

"*¡¿Qué pasa?!*" Joe shouted. "That cheese was for you!
"My bread," wailed his wife, "was a gift for you, too!"

Viv continued to moan, "Joe, my present's a wreck!"
Señor Joe answered grimly, "And mine looks like dreck!"

They doused out the fire using big water jugs;
Then they both sat with sad, tearful looks on their mugs

Till the smoke had died down, and their
   crying had, too.
  And then Viv said, "We both did the best
   we could do. . . ."

"And we did it with *love!*" Joe replied
   to his wife.
"It's the *thought* that counts, Viv!
   That's the meaning of life!"

Then they kissed one another,
   not saying a peep,
And they stumbled to bed and
   went straight back to sleep.

Now, don't think for a moment
   this story ends here,
'Cause young Olga—an orphan—
   was strolling quite near,

And because she was hungry, she snuck in and ate
A small bite of the cheese-goop, and cried, "This is great!"

Then she wolfed down some more, and took off down the street,
Shouting, "¡*Mira!* Come try this incredible treat!"

The neighbors all tried some; and then, with a roar,
They rushed, mouths wide open, to Joe and Viv's door.

"It's cheesy!" they hollered. "It's bready! It's tasty!"
"Please bake us some more, and we want it posthastey!"

Well, Viv and her husband awoke to this din,
and looked on, amazed, as the people poured in

And surrounded the happy, but overwhelmed, pair,
Waving moolah, *dinero*, and checks in the air.

"Bake more!" they kept chanting. "We need a new stash.
Bake more right now and we'll pay you—with cash!"

"¡*Te ayudo!*—I'll help you!" was Olga's reaction,
And Viv said, "Let's give her a piece of the action!"

The three kissed and hugged; then Joe said, with a wink,
"I *knew* this would happen!" And Viv said, "Just think . . .

The presents! The smoke! It was all meant to be!"
"Our troubles are over!" Joe answered with glee.

And so this odd trio became renowned bakers—
The pueblo's most popular cheese-and-bread makers!

Viv, Olga, and Joe gained both fortune and fame
And "Cheesybreadville" was declared the town's name!

But the cheesybread partners stayed humble, you know;
They counted their blessings (along with their dough).

And despite all they earned (a prodigious amount!),
They never forgot that good thoughts are what count.

And they also learned *this* (but please pardon the pun):
"When giving a present, make sure it's well-done!"

P.S.
Here is the recipe; give it a try.
It's easy to make; almost nothing to buy. . . .

But bake it with love, because this much I know:
You'll always be thrilled at how far love can go.

## CHEESYBREADVILLE CHEESE BREAD

Take one box of corn muffin mix. Follow the directions on the package, but add 1/2 cup of grated Parmesan cheese to the batter. Also mix in tons of good thoughts, and all the love and affection you can muster. Then bake (or burn) to your heart's content!

# SPLIT DECISION

By Matt Groening

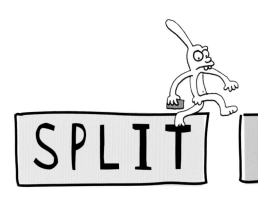

# I WANT IT

words and music by **Laurie Berkner**

illustrated by **Tom Lichtenheld**

(1.) I just got a brand-new bike and I love to ride it a-round.
(2.) I just got a brand-new drum and I love to play it loud.

I let my friends ride it to-day. At
I let my friends play it to-day. At

first it was o-kay, but then I felt a-fraid that
first it was o-kay, but then I felt a-fraid that

one of them would take my bike a-way. So I said,
one of them would take my drum a-way. So I said,

"Give it to me, give it to me, give it to me now! Give it to me, give it to me, give it to me now! 'Cause I

want it, I want it, and I've got to have it. I want it, I

want it now! Yes, I want it, I want it. I

can't bear to lose it. It's mine and I want it now."

Then it seemed that ev-'ry-thing was wrong.    I had my things, but all my friends were gone.    So

I went out all by my-self and rode my bike a-round, but this time when I played my drum, it made a lone-ly sound. 'Cause

(♩ = 74)

it was much more fun when my friends were there.___ Sud-den-ly I re-al-ized I want to share.___

We could bike to-geth-er, we could write a song.___ The drum can keep the beat, my friends-'ll sing a-long!___ We

(♩ = 124)

want it. (We need our friends.)___ We've got it. ('Cause in the end)___ It's

friend - ship___ that helps to see us through.___    We

want it. (The en-er-gy)___ We've got it. (of you and me.)___ To -

*Repeat and Fade*

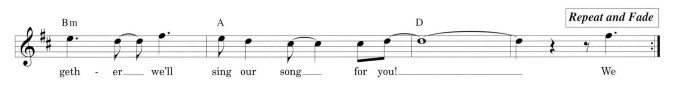
geth - er___ we'll sing our song___ for you!___    We

# THANK SOMEONE

Music by PAUL JACOBS
Words by SARAH DURKEE

# Thank Someone

*words by Sarah Durkee*
*music by Paul Jacobs*
*illustrated by Loren Long*

Mom put down the paper
just to help me find my shoe.
Kim likes chocolate doughnuts,
so her cousin gave her two.
Grampa played with Julio,
took him to the park.
If you forgot to thank someone,
say thank you in the dark.

Thank the moon,
thank the sun.
Most of all
thank someone.
Thank the stars
high above,
one for
everyone you love.

# GIVING

## A WHAT'S-MINE-IS-YOURS WORKSHEET FOR KIDS

**"INCLUDE YOUR CHILDREN WHEN YOU'RE TALKING ABOUT GIVING TO CHARITY. BRINGING KIDS INTO THE DISCUSSION SHOWS THEM THAT WE'RE ALL IN THIS TOGETHER." –DONALD TRUMP**

Keep three piggy banks in your room instead of just one. Then divide your money (whether it's your allowance, or a gift, or a reward for a chore you've done) this way:

**PIGGY BANK #1:** for spending on something to buy today (a CD?).

**PIGGY BANK #2:** for saving up for something expensive you really want (a bike?).

**PIGGY BANK #3:** for giving to help something you care about (the rain forest?).

**"MY FATHER DIDN'T HAVE THAT MUCH MONEY, BUT HE WAS A GENEROUS PERSON. HE TAUGHT ME THAT IF YOU DON'T HAVE MONEY, YOU CAN ALWAYS GIVE TIME." –TED TURNER**

Turn your favorite hobby into an act of giving.
• Do you enjoy riding your bike? Then volunteer to deliver groceries to someone in your neighborhood who is housebound.

• Do you like working outdoors? Why not help an elderly neighbor weed her garden?
• Are you a born performer? Put on a show in your backyard to raise money for an after-school program.

**"I BELIEVE THAT CHILDREN WHO HAVE A LOT SHOULD THINK ABOUT KIDS WHO DON'T HAVE AS MUCH. CHILDREN LEARN BY WATCHING THEIR PARENTS. WE CAN TEACH THEM HOW TO BE GENEROUS." –BARRY DILLER**

Next time Mom and Dad say to you, "What would you like for your birthday?" ask them if one present could be a contribution to a place where you can help make a difference. For example:
• an animal shelter. • the local science museum.
• a place <u>you</u> think of.

**"ASK YOUR CHILDREN TO MAKE A PILE OF ALL THE STUFF THEY NO LONGER USE. TELL THEM HOW MUCH IT ALL COST AND WHAT NEW THINGS THEY COULD BUY WITH THAT AMOUNT OF MONEY. THIS WILL HELP THEM BEGIN TO UNDERSTAND THE REAL VALUE OF A DOLLAR." –SUZE ORMAN**

ILLUSTRATED BY TOM LICHTENHELD

# THERE'S MORE THAN

## 1 WAY

### AND THEIR PARENTS

> "**CHILDREN SHOULD LEARN THAT THERE'S MORE TO LIFE THAN—YOU'LL EXCUSE THE BUSINESS TERM—THE BOTTOM LINE. I WAS RAISED TO BELIEVE THAT FOR EVERYTHING YOU'RE GIVEN, THERE'S ALWAYS SOMETHING TO GIVE BACK.**"
> **—SUMNER REDSTONE**

**W**henever you see something that makes you sad, don't get blue—get busy.

• If you feel bad about people who are homeless, find out where the nearest shelter is and volunteer.

• If you know a child who uses a wheelchair, offer to help that child find easy ways to get to places he or she would like to go.

• If you've outgrown some of your favorite stuff—clothing, toys, books—find a place in your neighborhood that collects things for kids who can use it.

> "**TEACHING A CHILD TO LEARN TO GIVE IS LIKE TEACHING SOMEONE A SONG—YOU HAVE TO SING IT FOR THEM FIRST. WE NEED TO SET THE EXAMPLE. AND IF WE'RE LUCKY, OUR KIDS WILL BRING BEAUTIFUL MUSIC INTO THE WORLD.**" **—DAVID GEFFEN**

**W**henever you see someone give time or money to help others, join in.

• If Mom is donating money to a cause, ask her whom it's for and how the money will help. Learn all about it.

• If Dad is lending his time to a local soup kitchen, tag along and tie on an apron. (Kids are allowed!)

• Log on to the internet. You're only a point-and-click away from finding out how to help a group whose work means something really special to you.

> "**STAY AWAY FROM CREDIT CARDS. IF I HAD BORROWED MONEY AT 18 PERCENT WHEN I WAS YOUNG, I'D BE IN THE POORHOUSE NOW.**"
> **—WARREN E. BUFFETT**

# CoNtRiBuToRs

**Nikki Anders** is a songwriter and performer; with the group Avalon, she has won five Dove Awards.

**Dan Andreasen** is the best-selling illustrator of picture books, including *A Quiet Place* and *A Special Day for Mommy,* which he also wrote.

**Avi** won the Newbery Award for his novel *Crispin: The Cross of Lead.* He has also received two Newbery Honors.

**Kevin Bacon** has appeared in such award-winning films as *Mystic River, Apollo 13, Animal House, Diner,* and *Footloose.*

**Michael Bacon** is an Emmy Award–winning composer for film and television. He and his brother, Kevin, formed the popular country-folk-rock group, The Bacon Brothers.

**Joseph A. Bailey** is best known for his writing contributions to *Sesame Street, The Muppet Show,* and such television specials as *Big Bird in China* and *Rocky Mountain Holiday.*

**Robin Batteau** is an award-winning songwriter, singer, and violin soloist.

**Laurie Berkner** is known for her best-selling albums *Under a Shady Tree* and *Victor Vito,* the latter of which was adapted as a picture book featuring Henry Cole's illustrations.

**Harry Bliss** is an award-winning cartoonist and cover artist for the *New Yorker* and the illustrator of books for children.

**Sarah S. Brannen** has been a painter and an architectural illustrator; she now writes and illustrates children's books.

**Mel Brooks** is the writer and director of *The Producers* (for which he won an Academy Award), *Young Frankenstein,* and *Blazing Saddles.* His stage adaptation of *The Producers* won an unprecedented twelve Tony Awards.

**Marc Brown** is the creator of the beloved aardvark Arthur, about whom he's written thirty books and developed a celebrated PBS television series.

**Warren E. Buffett** is a value investor and the CEO of Berkshire Hathaway, Inc.

**Eric Carle** is the author and illustrator of many books, including the modern classic *The Very Hungry Caterpillar,* which has sold more than 10 million copies.

**David Catrow** is the illustrator of numerous books for children, several of them *New York Times* Best Illustrated Books.

**Christopher Cerf** has won five Emmy and two Grammy Awards for his writing,

composing, and producing contributions to *Sesame Street, The Electric Company, Free to Be . . . a Family,* and *Between the Lions,* the highly acclaimed literacy education series he co-created for PBS.

**Tom Chapin** is a two-time Grammy Award–winning singer-songwriter. His popular albums for children and grown-ups have also received honors from the American Library Association, the Parents' Choice Foundation, and *Parents* magazine.

**Deepak Chopra** has been heralded by *Time* magazine as the "poet-philosopher of alternative medicine" and one of the "top one hundred icons of the century." He has written more than twenty-five books, which have been translated into thirty-five languages.

**R. Gregory Christie** has twice received the Coretta Scott King Honor for his children's book illustrations.

**Henry Cole** has illustrated numerous books, including *The Sissy Duckling* by Harvey Fierstein and *Little Bo* by Julie Andrews Edwards.

**Demi** is the author and illustrator of many children's books, including *Gandhi,* which was a *New York Times* Best Illustrated Picture Book.

**Kate DiCamillo** is the author of the 2004 Newbery Medal winner, *The Tale of Despereaux, The Tiger Rising,* and *Because of Winn-Dixie,* a Newbery Honor Book.

**Barry Diller** is chairman and CEO of IAC/InterActiveCorp.

**Hilary Duff** is an actress and a singer who starred in *Lizzie McGuire,* recorded a number-one solo album, and has several popular movies to her credit.

**Sarah Durkee** is a multiple–Emmy Award–winning script- and songwriter. Her credits include *Sesame Street, Between the Lions, Free to Be . . . a Family,* and several popular recordings by Meat Loaf.

**Delia Ephron** is an author, a screenwriter, and a producer whose credits include *Sleepless in Seattle, You've Got Mail,* and *Michael.*

**Ken Feisel** is the art director of *Archaeology* magazine. His work has also appeared in *People* and *TV Guide.*

**John Forster** has written and produced a number of award-winning albums and multiplatinum music videos.

**Phil Galdston**'s song "Save the Best for Last" reached #1 on *Billboard*'s three major charts and was named ASCAP's Song of the Year.

**David Geffen** founded the Asylum and Geffen record labels, and cofounded DreamWorks SKG.

**Larry Gelbart** has been one of America's most acclaimed comedy writers for more than fifty years. Among his credits are *M\*A\*S\*H, Tootsie, Sid Caesar's Show of Shows,* and *A Funny Thing Happened on the Way to the Forum.*

**Whoopi Goldberg** has won the Grammy, the Academy Award, the Golden Globe, the Emmy, and the Tony and has been honored with NAACP Image, People's Choice, and Nickelodeon Kids' Choice awards.

**Matt Groening** is the creator and executive producer of the Emmy Award–winning show *The Simpsons.* His other projects include the "Life in Hell" comics and *Futurama.*

**Carol Hall** has been a major contributor to *Sesame Street* and *Free to Be . . . You and Me.* Her songs have been recorded by Marlo Thomas, Harry Belafonte, Barbra Streisand, Dolly Parton, and Tony Bennett, among others.

**Sheldon Harnick** is a Tony-, Grammy-, and Pulitzer Prize–winning writer who composed the lyrics for *Fiddler on the Roof* and *She Loves Me.*

**Bruce Hart,** one of the first writers on *Sesame Street,* co-created *Free to Be . . . You and Me* with Marlo Thomas and served as head writer for the Emmy-winning TV special.

**Paul Jacobs** is the music director for *Between the Lions.* He has also won Emmy Awards and platinum records for his collaborations with pop artists.

**Karen Katz** is a fine artist who has written and illustrated several books, including *Counting Kisses, Twelve Hats for Lena,* and *Where Is Baby's Belly Button?*

**Bruce Kluger** serves on the board of contributors for *USA Today,* and his writing has appeared in *Parenting* magazine, *Newsweek,* the *New York Times,* the *Los Angeles Times,* and on National Public Radio.

**Lisa Kopelke** has written and illustrated the books *Excuse Me!* and *Tissue, Please!,* both about manners.

**Ed Koren** has illustrated books by Delia Ephron and Peter Mayle and is a cartoonist for the *New Yorker.*

**Gail Carson Levine** is the author of many successful children's books, including the Newbery Honor Book *Ella Enchanted.*

**Tom Lichtenheld** has written and illustrated several books for children, including *Everything I Know About Cars.*

LOREN LONG is the illustrator of Madonna's book *Mr. Peabody's Apples* as well as the Golden Kite Award–winning *I Dream of Trains* by Angela Johnson.

SONIA MANZANO has starred as "Maria" on *Sesame Street* for more than thirty years and has earned fifteen Emmys as a member of the program's writing staff.

JIM MARR is a songwriter, guitarist, and record producer who has helped create platinum-selling songs and albums for such artists as Hilary Duff, Billie Piper, and Martine McCutcheon.

JOE MATHIEU has illustrated more than one hundred books, most notably for *Sesame Street,* and in collaboration with best-selling author Laura Numeroff.

CHARLIE MIDNIGHT has three Grammy Award–winning albums, a Grammy-nominated song, and two Golden Globe–nominated films to his credit.

JULIANNE MOORE has been nominated for the Academy Award and the Golden Globe. She has appeared in such films as *Far from Heaven, The Hours,* and *Boogie Nights.*

JEFF MOSS was one of the original creators of *Sesame Street,* in connection with which he earned fifteen Emmys. His first published poem, "The Entertainer," appeared in *Free to Be . . . a Family* and launched him on a second career as a best-selling children's poet. He died in 1998.

FRANKIE MUNIZ is the Emmy- and Golden Globe Award–nominated star of the long-running series *Malcolm in the Middle.* His feature film credits include *My Dog Skip, Big Fat Liar,* and *Agent Cody Banks.*

JON J MUTH's illustrations appear in the children's books *The Three Questions* and *Come On, Rain!* by Newbery Award winner Karen Hesse.

CHRISTOPHER MYERS received the Caldecott Honor for illustrating *Harlem,* which was written by his father, Walter Dean Myers.

WALTER DEAN MYERS has received the Coretta Scott King Award four times as well as two Newbery Honors and the Margaret A. Edwards Award.

JOSEPH S. NEWMAN made his living selling sporting goods with his brother Arthur, Paul Newman's father. He was a journalist for the Cleveland *Plain Dealer* and the *Cleveland Press* and wrote and taught poetry, which has been collected in several volumes.

PAUL NEWMAN has appeared in fifty-one films and four Broadway plays. All of the profits from his successful food conglomerate are given to charity.

SUZE ORMAN, personal finance author and television personality, is the author of four consecutive *New York Times* best-sellers.

WENDY PAGE is a singer, songwriter, and producer who has worked on three number-one albums and six top-five singles in Britain and America.

ROSIE PEREZ has appeared in such films as *Do the Right Thing, White Men Can't Jump,* and *Fearless,* for which she earned an Oscar nomination. She also works with organizations including the Latino Commission on AIDS and the Working Playground, an arts program for public schools.

JIMMY PICKERING's unique artistic style has earned him major assignments from Hallmark, The Walt Disney Company, and Universal Studios. He has illustrated several picture books, including *It's Fall* and *It's Winter,* both of which he also wrote.

JERRY PINKNEY is the acclaimed illustrator of four Caldecott Honor Books, two of which also received Coretta Scott King Honors.

ELISE PRIMAVERA's artwork can be seen in a number of books for children, including the Auntie Claus books, which she both wrote and illustrated.

SUMNER REDSTONE is the chairman of Viacom, the media company behind entertainment businesses such as Paramount Pictures, MTV, Nickelodeon, Blockbuster, and Simon & Schuster.

RAY ROMANO is the star of the long-running series *Everybody Loves Raymond,* for which he has been honored with the People's Choice, Emmy, American Comedy, and Viewers for Quality Television awards. His feature film credits include *Ice Age* and *Welcome to Mooseport.*

BARRY ROOT has illustrated a number of children's books. *Someplace Else* was named a Best Illustrated Book by the *New York Times.*

S. D. SCHINDLER has illustrated many popular books, among them, *How Santa Got His Job, How Santa Lost His Job,* and *Skeleton Hiccups.*

JON SCIESZKA is the author of such best-selling titles as *The Stinky Cheese Man* and *Math Curse.*

MAURICE SENDAK has written and illustrated more than eighty books for children. He received the Caldecott Medal for *Where the Wild Things Are* and was honored with the International Hans Christian Andersen Medal for Illustration and the Laura Ingalls Wilder Award.

DAVID SHANNON's books for children include the Caldecott Honor Book *No, David!; How Georgie Radbourn Saved Baseball,* a *New York Times* Best Illustrated Book; and *The Amazing Christmas Extravaganza,* an ABA Kids' Pick of the Lists.

SHEL SILVERSTEIN wrote and illustrated several best-selling children's classics, including *Where the Sidewalk Ends, A Light in the Attic,* and *The Giving Tree.* His stories appeared in the *Free to Be . . . You and Me* and *Free to Be . . . a Family* books, records, and television shows. He died in 1999.

DAVID SLAVIN's cultural and political satire has been featured in the *New York Times,* the *Los Angeles Times,* Salon.com, and on National Public Radio's "All Things Considered."

LANE SMITH is known for his illustrations for the Caldecott Honor Book *The Stinky Cheese Man* and *The True Story of the Three Little Pigs,* both by Jon Scieszka.

NORMAN STILES is the former head writer of *Sesame Street* and co-creator of the PBS television series *Between the Lions.* The winner of twelve Emmy Awards, he has authored and coauthored numerous children's books.

MARC SWERSKY is a songwriter and producer who has worked with artists including Joe Cocker and Hilary Duff.

DONALD TRUMP is a real estate developer who has owned a number of key properties, including the Trump Towers, Trump Plaza, and the Plaza Hotel, as well as Atlantic City casinos such as the Taj Majal.

TED TURNER is the founder of Turner Broadcasting Systems. He directs most of his philanthropic activities through Turner Foundation, Inc., of which he is chairman; the United Nations Foundation; and the Nuclear Threat Initiative.

GERALDO VALÉRIO has published several children's books in Brazil and Portugal. *Do You Have a Hat?* by Eileen Spinelli is the first English-language book he has illustrated.

WENDY WASSERSTEIN won the Pulitzer Prize for her play *The Heidi Chronicles.* Wendy's daughter, Lucy Jane, provided artwork for her mom's story in *Thanks & Giving.*

MO WILLEMS is a six-time Emmy Award winner and the recipient of the Caldecott Honor for *Don't Let the Pigeon Drive the Bus!,* which he wrote and illustrated.

TIGER WOODS was the first person to hold all four professional major golf championships at the same time. By winning the British Open, Woods became the youngest golfer to complete the career Grand Slam of professional major championships.

PAUL O. ZELINSKY won the Caldecott Medal for *Rapunzel* and received three Caldecott Honors: for *Hansel and Gretel, Rumpelstiltskin,* and *Swamp Angel.*

# ABOUT ST. JUDE CHILDREN'S RESEARCH HOSPITAL

Moms, dads, and kids come to St. Jude from cities and towns everywhere. They come from communities all across the United States and from countries all over the world so that our heroic teams of doctors and scientists can help them in their battle to overcome cancer and other dangerous diseases.

Many of these diseases used to be a mystery. Where did they come from? How did they happen? Why do some children get so sick, and what can be done to help them?

Today our scientists at St. Jude are solving many of these mysteries. In fact, sickness, and curing it, is *all about* science. Cancer, for example, is about cells in our bodies that aren't working right. So we're doing research at St. Jude to find new ways to repair these cells, or even prevent them from going wrong in the first place.

That's why our name has always been St. Jude Children's *Research* Hospital.

St. Jude is such a special place, for so many families, in so many ways. No family ever has to pay for the treatment they receive at St. Jude if they cannot afford it. The costs of their care, their medications, and even their travel and housing are fully covered, no matter how far they have to come, or how long they have to stay.

And just as moms, dads, and kids come to St. Jude from all over, our scientific discoveries are shared with doctors and hospitals everywhere—including in *your* community. That means the work we do at St. Jude is free to *everyone*.

You're helping too. How? By owning this book, since all of its royalties go to support the work at St. Jude. There are other ways to be a part of St. Jude, too:

- You can join in a St. Jude Math-A-Thon® at your school or a Bike-A-Thon™ in your hometown—both of which support St. Jude.
- You can visit us at our St. Jude Web site, meet our Patient of the Month, and learn about his or her challenges and hopes.
- You can do your own research at our Web site, learning as much as you'd like about the great progress our scientists are making on the frontiers of medical science.
- There's even a special kids' Web page, where you can share with us some of *your* ideas about how to help the children of St. Jude.

I hope you and your family will visit us soon at www.stjude.org.

*With Love,*
*The scientists, doctors, nurses —*
*and the kids — of St. Jude*